7-16-16

THE
COSTARELLA
CONQUEST

THE COSTARELLA CONQUEST

BY

EMMA DARCY

First published in Great Britain 2011
by Mills & Boon, an imprint of Harlequin (UK) Limited.
Large Print edition 2012
Harlequin (UK) Limited, Eton House,
18-24 Paradise Road, Richmond, Surrey TW9 1SR

© Emma Darcy 2011

ISBN: 978 0 263 22551 8

Printed and bound in Great Britain
by CPI Antony Rowe, Chippenham, Wiltshire

CHAPTER ONE

FRIDAY afternoon in the office of the man Jake Freedman had every reason to hate, and he could barely contain his impatience to leave. Soon, very soon, he would have all the evidence to indict Alex Costarella for the vulture he was, picking over the carcasses of bankrupted companies to feed his own bankroll. Then he could leave for good. In the meantime, the facade of aspiring to be Costarella's right-hand man in the liquidation business could not afford any cracks.

'It's Mother's Day on Sunday,' the big man remarked, eyeing Jake with speculative interest. 'You don't have any family, do you?'

Not since you helped to kill my stepfather.

Jake managed a rueful smile. 'Lost both my parents in my teens.'

'Yes, I remember you saying so. Difficult for you. Makes it all the more admirable that you pushed on with a career path and have made such a fine job of it.'

Every step of the way had been burning with the ambition to take this man down. And he would. It had taken ten years to get to this point—accountancy, law, building up experience in Costarella's business, gaining his confidence. Only a few more months now...

'I'd like you to meet my daughter.'

Shock startled Jake out of his secret brooding and rattled his ruthless determination. He'd never thought about the vulture's family, or what effect his own actions might have on them. He raised his eyebrows enquiringly. Was the daughter about to come into her father's business or...was this some weird attempt at matchmaking?

'Laura is a stunner in any man's language. Smart girl and a great cook,' Costarella declared with an inviting smile. 'Come to lunch at my home on Sunday and find out for yourself.'

A sales pitch! And a set-up for a connection to be made!

Jake inwardly recoiled from an up-close-and-personal involvement with anyone related to this man. His hand moved instinctively in a negative gesture. 'I'd be intruding on your family day.'

'I want you to come, Jake.'

The expression on his face brooked no refusal. It was a strong, handsome face, framed by thick, steel-grey hair and dominated by steel-grey eyes—a face imbued with the confidence of a man who could and did take control of anything and bend it to his will.

Jake knew instantly that if he persisted in declining the invitation, the approval rating that gave him access to the evidence he needed could be lost. 'That's very kind of you,' he rolled out with an appreciative smile. 'If you're sure I'd be welcome...'

Any doubt on that score was clearly irrelevant. What Costarella wanted, he got. 'Make it eleven-thirty,' he said without hesitation. 'You know where I live?'

'Yes. Thank you. I'll look forward to it.'

'Good! I'll see you then.' The grey eyes glittered with satisfaction. 'You won't be disappointed.'

Jake nodded, taking his dismissal as gracefully as he could, knowing he had to turn up on Sunday, knowing he had to show an interest in *the daughter*, and hating the idea with every fibre of his being.

Why Costarella wanted this, he didn't know. It seemed ridiculously patriarchal in this day and age to be lining up a suitor, as though people were pawns to be moved as he wished. Nevertheless, it was typical of the callous mentality of the man. He moved to his own beat, not giving a damn about anyone else's interests.

Jake had to go along with him, play for time, protect his own agenda. If he had to start dating Laura Costarella he would, but no way would he allow himself to become emotionally attached to her, regardless of how beautiful and smart she was.

She was the daughter of the enemy.

He wasn't about to forget that.

Ever.

Mother's Day...

Laura Costarella wished it could be what it was supposed to be—a beautiful, memorable day for her mother with her children showing their love and appreciation for all she'd done for them, and their father being happy with the family they'd created together.

It wasn't going to be like that.

Her father had invited a special guest to the

family lunch and from the smug little smile accompanying this announcement, Laura strongly suspected that the guest would be used to show up the shortcomings in his son and daughter, as well as the failings of the mother who had raised them.

Jake Freedman—a hard name, and undoubtedly as hard in character as her father was, or he wouldn't have risen so fast to the top of the tree in the Costarella Accountancy Company, which raked in millions from bankrupt firms. Did he know how he was going to be used today? Did he care?

Laura shook her head over the futile speculation. What would happen would happen. She couldn't stop it. All she could do was cook her mother's favourite foods for lunch and try to deflect the barbs of her father's discontent with his family. Keep smiling, she told herself, no matter what.

She hoped her brother would follow that

advice today, too, for their mother's sake. No eruption into a resentful rage. No walking out. Just smile and shrug off any critical remarks like water off a duck's back. Surely it wasn't too much to ask for Eddie to keep his testosterone in check for one short day.

The doorbell rang as she finished preparing the vegetables for baking as she'd seen done on the cooking show that was one of her favourite television programs. They were ready to slip into the oven with the slowly roasting leg of lamb when the time was right. The pumpkin and bacon soup only had to be reheated. The cream was whipped and the lemon-lime tart was in the refrigerator waiting to be served.

She quickly washed her hands, removed her apron and pasted a smile on her face, determined to greet their visitor with all the charm she could muster.

Jake stood at the front door to Alex Costarella's Mosman mansion, steeling himself to be an appreciative and charming guest. The huge two-storey redbrick home was one of Sydney's old establishment houses, set in immaculately kept grounds, oozing solid respectability—a perfect front to hide the true nature of the man who had acquired it by ripping off other people.

He remembered how hard his stepfather had fought the bankruptcy officials to hold back the sale of their family home while his mother was still alive—just a few more months until the cancer finally took her. No caring, no mercy from the money men. And the whole rotten process had been started by Costarella, who had deliberately turned a blind eye to how a company and hundreds of jobs could have been saved, preferring the prospect of lining his own pockets while being in charge of selling off all the assets.

No caring, no mercy.

His stepfather's heart had given out only a few weeks after his mother had died. Two funerals in close succession. Jake couldn't lay both of them at Costarella's door, but he could certainly lay one. It amused him to think of himself as the wolf outside, waiting to be given open entry to another wolf's home.

Taronga Park Zoo was nearby.

But the dangerous animals were right here.

Costarella didn't know Jake was on the prowl, waiting for the right moment to attack. He was holding his daughter out as bait for a bright future with the young gun in the company, unaware that *he* was the targeted prey. As for Laura, herself…

The door opened and Jake was faced with a woman who instantly excited an interest. She *was* beautiful; long black curly hair, incredible blue eyes, a mouth with lush full lips stretched into a greeting smile of perfect white teeth. She wore a clingy top in purple and white, the neckline dipping down low enough to reveal the upper swell of breasts that were more than big enough to fill a man's hands. Tight purple jeans outlined the rest of her hourglass figure and emphasised the seductive length of her shapely legs. The sexual animal inside Jake growled with the desire to take.

It was several moments before he recovered wits enough to identify himself as the expected guest. 'I'm Jake. Jake Freedman,' he said, hoping she hadn't noticed how *taken* he was by her.

Alex Costarella's daughter was a man-trap.

Falling into it did not fit into his plan.

'Hello. I'm Laura, the daughter of the house.'

She heard herself say the words as though from a great distance, her mind totally stunned by how handsome Jake Freedman was. Though *handsome* didn't say it all, not by a long shot. She'd met a lot of good-looking men. Her brother's world was full of them, actors making their mark in television shows. But this man…

what was it that had her heart racing and her
stomach fluttering?

His hair was dark brown and cut so short
the wave in it was barely noticeable. Somehow the lack of careful styling made his dark
brown eyes more riveting. Or maybe it was
the unusual shape of them, his eyelids droop-
ing in a way that made them look triangular
and incredibly sexy. A strong straight nose, a
strong squarish jaw and a strongly sculptured
mouth added to the male impact of his face. He
would have been perfectly cast as James Bond,
Laura thought, and had the nervous feeling he
was just as dangerous as the legendary 007
character.

He had the physique to go with it, too. As tall
as her father but more lethally lean and looking
powerfully masculine in his black jeans and
black-and-white sports shirt, the long sleeves
casually rolled up to the elbows, revealing
hard muscular forearms. Jake Freedman was

so male, it was stirring everything female in her. Even though she knew he was her father's man, it was impossible not to feel interested in him.

'Pleased to meet you,' he said, offering his hand with a smile that made him even sexier.

'Likewise,' Laura replied, extending her own hand and finding it subjected to an electric sensation that was so shocking she wanted to snatch it away. 'Please come in,' she rattled out, needing movement to excuse the quick extraction from physical contact with him.

'Daughter of the house,' he repeated musingly as he stepped inside. 'Does that mean you still live here at home?'

The curious assessment in his eyes gave her the sense he was summing up possibilities between them. 'Yes. It's a big house,' she answered drily. Big enough to keep out of her father's way most of the time.

Jake Freedman had to be years older than

her university friends, given his position in her father's business, and remembering that unpleasant fact she should avoid him like the plague, apart from getting through this visit today. They would have nothing—absolutely nothing—in common.

'The family is enjoying the sunshine on the back patio,' she said, leading him down the wide hallway that bisected the house. 'I'll take you out to Dad, then bring you some refreshments. What would you like to drink?'

'A glass of iced water would be fine, thank you.'

It surprised her. 'Not a Scotch on the rocks man like my father?'

'No.'

'What about a vodka martini?'

'Just water.'

Well, he wasn't James Bond, she thought, swallowing down a silly giggle.

'Do you have a job, Laura?'

'Yes, I'm a Director of First Impressions.' It was okay to let the laughter gurgle out at his puzzled expression. 'I read it in the newspaper this morning,' she explained. 'It's the title now given to a receptionist.'

'Ah!' He smiled at the pretentiousness of it.

'You know what they call a window cleaner?'

'Please enlighten me.'

'A vision clearance executive.'

He laughed, making his megawatt attractiveness zoom even higher.

'A teacher is a knowledge navigator,' Laura rattled on, trying to ignore his effect on her. 'And a librarian is an information retrieval specialist. I can't remember the rest of the list. All the titles were very wordy.'

'So putting it simply, you're a receptionist.'

'Part-time at a local medical practice. I'm still at uni, doing landscape architecture. It's a four-year degree program and I'm currently making my way through the last year.'

'Working and studying? Your father doesn't support you?' he queried, obviously not quite in tune with a wealthy man who wouldn't finance his children's full education.

She slanted him a derisive look. 'My father doesn't support what he doesn't approve of. You should know that since you work with him.'

'But you're his daughter.'

'Who was expected to fall in with his wishes. I'm allowed to live here. That's as much support as my father will give to my career choice.'

'Perhaps you should have sought complete independence.'

It was an odd remark, coming from a man who had to have made an art form of falling in with her father's wishes. However, she wasn't about to discuss the dynamics of her family with an outsider, particularly not someone who specialised in siding with her father.

'My mother needs me.'

It was a brief reply and all he was going to get from her. She opened the back door and ushered him out to the patio, quickly announcing, 'Your Jake is here, Dad.'

'Ah!' Her father rose from his chair at the patio table, which was strewn with the Sunday newspapers. His whole face beamed a welcome at the man who was undoubtedly performing up to his expectations in every respect. 'Good to see you here, Jake. Beautiful autumn day, isn't it?'

'Couldn't be better,' he agreed, moving forward to shake her father's offered hand.

Confident, smooth, at ease with himself and the situation…and Laura definitely wasn't. She felt dreadfully at odds with the strong tug of attraction that wouldn't go away. It was wrong. It had to be wrong. The last thing she wanted was a man like her father messing with her life.

'Go and fetch your mother, Laura. She's showing Eddie the latest innovations in the garden. You can tell them both to come and meet our guest.'

'Will do,' she said, glad to leave the two men together, though knowing that the stirring of the family pot couldn't be delayed for long. Her father expected instant obedience to his call.

The garden was her mother's refuge. She was never happier than when discussing what could be done next to it with Nick Jeffries, the handyman who shared her enthusiasm for creating wonderful visual effects and did all the heavy work for her. Laura loved this garden, too, loved every aspect of landscape design, making something beautiful instead of tearing something down…as her father did.

And as Jake Freedman did.

It would be stupid to forget that. She could never, never be in tune with a mind that dealt with destruction.

'Mum, Eddie…' she called out. They were

by the rockpool, where Nick had installed the new solar lights. 'Dad's guest is here.'

Her mother's smile of pleasure instantly drooped into a grimace. She darted an anxious look at her son, worried about an imminent clash of personalities.

Eddie hugged her shoulders, smiling reassurance. 'I promise I'll be good, Mum. No bad boy today.'

It won a wry little laugh.

Eddie made a great *bad boy* in the soap opera he currently starred in. The wild flop of his thick black hair, the designer stubble along his angular jawline, the dimple in his chiselled chin, the piercing blue eyes…all made him a very popular pin-up, especially on his flash motorbike. He was wearing black leathers today, though he was now carrying his jacket, discarded because of the heat of the morning. His white T-shirt was emblazoned with a

Harley-Davidson. He played a bikie and he looked like one, much to her father's disgust.

The three of them started strolling back towards the patio, son and daughter flanking their mother, determined to keep a happy ball rolling for her. Why she stayed with their father was beyond their comprehension. There was no joy in the marriage. Having a very dominant husband who controlled everything seemed to have sapped her of any will for an independent life.

Laura always thought of her mother as a lady, never anything but beautifully dressed and groomed, imbued with gracious manners, doing everything correctly and tastefully, making a special ritual of keeping fresh floral arrangements in the house, which she did herself. Even her name, Alicia, was somehow very ladylike.

She looked particularly lovely today, her newly dyed blond hair cut into a short, fluffy style, a blue silk tunic giving her eyes more colour. They had seemed so dull and washed out lately, Laura had worried there might be a health problem her mother was not admitting to. She was getting too thin, as well, a fact hidden by the loosely fitting long-sleeved tunic. The white slacks were also loose, affecting a casually elegant look. Certainly no one would notice anything amiss with her, not on the surface. Jake Freedman would probably pigeonhole her as the typical rich man's wife.

'What's he like?' her mother asked.

'James Bond,' popped straight out of Laura's mouth.

'What? Loaded and dangerous?' Eddie queried.

She grinned at him. 'Plus gorgeous and sexy.'

He rolled his eyes. 'Don't you go falling for him, Laura. That's bad territory.'

'Yes, be careful,' her mother quickly warned,

her eyes anxious again. 'Your father might want you to like this man. There has to be some motive behind inviting him here today.'

'Could be that marrying the boss's daughter is on Jake Freedman's agenda,' Eddie put in, grinning wolfishly, then snapping his teeth to make the point.

Marriage?

Never!

She'd walked out of every relationship she'd had once the guy started making demands on her, which always happened sooner or later. From what she'd witnessed at home, marriage was an endless string of demands, plus abuse thrown in if the demands weren't met. No man was ever going to own her as his wife.

She rolled her eyes back at Eddie. 'I'm not so easy to gobble up. I'll be feeding him lunch. He can whistle for anything more from me.'

'Humphrey Bogart,' her mother murmured.

'What?'

'Humphrey Bogart. He whistled for Lauren Bacall. It was in an old movie.'

'Well, I haven't seen it.'

'Did he get her in the end?' Eddie asked.

'Yes.'

'No doubt she wanted to be got,' Laura said, giving her brother a quelling look. 'Different story.'

'I'll be watching the mouth of Dad's man of the moment,' he tossed back at her, wicked teasing in his eyes. 'If he starts whistling…'

'It's more likely the man of the moment is about to be used to show you up as a footloose lightweight, Eddie, so watch your own mouth.'

'I don't know…I don't know…' their mother fretted.

'It's okay, Mum,' Eddie quickly soothed. 'Laura and I have put our walls up and nothing is going to crack them today. Just you relax now. We're both on guard.'

It was a relief to hear Eddie so sure that his protective armour was in place. Laura wished she could say the same for herself. Despite what her mind dictated, as soon as they came into view of the two men on the patio and she caught Jake Freedman's gaze on her, there was no wall at all to hold off the sexual chemistry he triggered in her.

Immediately she felt a wild tingling in her breasts, shooting her nipples into hard bullets. Her hips started swaying provocatively, driven by some primitive instinct to show off her femininity. Heat whooshed to the apex of her thighs and somehow melted the normal strength in her legs. Her toes curled. And turbulent temptation crashed through every bit of common sense that told her to keep away from this man.

She would love to have him.

Regardless of how wrong it would be.
She would love to have him.
Just for the experience!

CHAPTER TWO

JAKE found it difficult to tear his gaze away from Laura to make a quick assessment of the other two people he was about to meet. The mother was more or less what he expected of Alex Costarella's wife—a lady-of-the-manor type who undoubtedly kept his house as beautifully as she kept herself—but the son was a surprise...unkempt, longish black hair, designer stubble, clothes indicative of a bikie. Obviously Eddie didn't toe his father's line, either.

Two rebellious children and one submissive wife.

Was he supposed to tame Laura, draw her into becoming the kind of woman her father would approve of, sharing his world instead of striking out on her own, pleasing herself?

He looked at her again and felt a tightening in his groin. She was, without a doubt, the most desirable woman he'd ever come into contact with, dangerous to play with, yet the idea of drawing her *away* from her father made her all the more tempting. It was fair justice for Costarella to feel the loss of someone dear to him as well as the loss of the business that gave him the power to wreck people's lives.

He was acutely aware of Laura watching him as her father performed the introductions, weighing up how he responded to her family.

'Alicia, my wife…'

'Delighted to meet you,' Jake rolled out with a smile.

She returned it but there was a wary look in her eyes as she replied, 'Welcome to our home.'

'And my son, Eddie, who obviously didn't

bother to shave this morning, not even for his mother.'

The acid criticism was brushed off with a nonchalant grin. 'Couldn't do it, Dad. We're shooting tomorrow. Got to stay in character.' He turned the grin to Jake as he offered his hand. 'I guess you're the son my father should have had, Jake. Happy days, man!'

Jake laughed and took his hand, shaking his head as he replied, 'Don't know about that but thanks for the good wishes, Eddie.'

'You're welcome.'

'Eddie is an actor,' Laura put in proudly. 'He plays the bad boy in *The Wild and the Wonderful*.'

Jake frowned apologetically. 'I'm sorry. I don't know the show.'

Her father snorted. 'It's rubbish. A TV soapie.'

'Rubbish or not, I enjoy doing it,' Eddie declared, totally unabashed. 'How about you, Jake? Do you enjoy doing what you do?'

'It's challenging. I guess acting is, too,' he said, careful to be even-handed in his reply.

'Totally absurd la-la-land,' Costarella jeered. 'Jake and I deal with the real world, Eddie.'

'Well, Dad, lots of people like to have a break from the real world and I help give it to them.' He deftly turned attention back to the guest. 'How do you relax from the pressure-cooker of work, Jake?'

Jake found himself liking Laura's brother. He stood up for himself and was clearly his own man. 'Something physical does the trick for me,' he answered.

'Yeah, got to say sex does it for me, too,' Eddie drawled, eyes twinkling with reckless mischief.

'Eddie!'

The shocked cry from his mother brought a swift apology. 'Sorry, Mum. It's all Laura's fault, saying Jake was sexy.'

'Did she now?' Costarella said with satisfaction.

'Eddie!' Laura cried in exasperation. 'I told you to watch your mouth.'

Jake turned to her, curious to see the reaction to her brother's claim. Her eyes were flashing furious sparks and her cheeks were flushed with embarrassment. As she met his gaze, her chin tilted defiantly and her own tongue let loose.

'Don't look at me as though you haven't heard that about yourself before because I bet you have. It's purely an observation, not an invitation.'

'Laura!' Another shocked protest from the mother.

She threw up her hands. 'Sorry, Mum. I'm off to bring out refreshments. Iced water coming up.'

Jake couldn't help grinning as she turned tail—a very sexy tail—and left the rest of them to patch a conversation together.

'I did try to bring my children up with good manners,' Alicia stated with a heavy sigh.

'No harm done,' her husband declared cheerfully.

'Actually, I like working out at a gym,' Jake said to remove sex from everyone's minds.

''Course you do,' Eddie chimed in. 'Can't get those muscles from sitting at a desk.'

'I do a yoga class,' Alicia offered, anxious to promote non-contentious chat as she gestured for everyone to sit down, tidying the newspapers on the table before sitting down herself.

Jake hadn't expected to find himself interested in Costarella's family. Even less had he expected to *like* any of them. In fact, the only one he'd given any thought to was Laura, whom he'd imagined to be a pampered princess, revelling in the role of Daddy's little girl.

The family dynamics were certainly intriguing and Jake was not averse to exploring them further...watching, listening, gathering information…and maybe, maybe, he might go after what he wanted with Laura Costarella, satisfying himself on several levels.

Laura cursed Eddie for being provocative, cursed herself for reacting so wildly, cursed Jake Freedman for making her feel stuff that completely rocked any sensible composure. Her escape to the kitchen should have settled her nerves but they were still jumping all over the place even after she'd loaded the traymobile with the preferred drinks and the platter of hors d'oeuvres.

There was no hiding from the man. He had to be faced again. She could only hope he wouldn't try capitalising on her remark or she'd be severely tempted to pour the jug of iced water over his head. Which just went to show how out of control she was and that just wouldn't do. Better to freeze him off with good manners. She had to keep remembering that

Jake Freedman was her father's man and any close connection with him could not lead anywhere good.

Not emotionally.

No matter how good he might be in bed.

And she had to stop thinking of that, too.

Having taken several deep breaths and gritting her teeth with determination to behave as she should, Laura wheeled the traymobile out to the patio. It was a relief to find the four of them chatting amicably about relaxation techniques; meditation, Tai Chi, massage and flotation tanks. Even her father appeared to be in good humour. She noted glumly that the only empty chair left for her at the round table was between Jake Freedman and her mother so she couldn't avoid being physically close to the man.

She set the platter on the table for everyone to help themselves, handed the ice-bucket containing a bottle of her mother's favourite white wine to Eddie and told him to open it, placed the jug of iced water and a crystal tumbler in front of Jake, served her father his Scotch on the rocks, and supplied the wineglasses before bowing to the inevitable of taking the designated chair and addressing the gaffe she'd made.

'I'm sorry for blowing my stack with you, Jake. I was annoyed with Eddie. And embarrassed.'

The riveting brown eyes sparkled with amusement, making her stomach flutter again. 'No offence taken, Laura. I dare say Eddie hears that said about himself so often, it's lost any currency with him. And I doubt he thought it had any currency with me, either.'

Letting her know he didn't have tickets on himself, not on that score anyway. Though Laura wasn't sure she believed him.

Her father snorted in rank disbelief. 'If it didn't have any currency with Eddie, he'd be out of a job. It's only because all the teeny-boppers think he's sexy that he's built up a fan base.'

'Lucky for me!' Eddie said flippantly. 'Though I do work at it, Dad.'

'Some people just have it,' her mother said, trying to divert a clash. 'I always thought Sean Connery…'

'Back to James Bond,' Eddie cut in, grinning at Laura.

She bared her teeth at him in warning.

He stood up to pour the wine, cheerfully saying, 'Mum's a great movie buff, Jake. I bet no one could beat her on that topic in a quiz show. And she's a champion Mum, too. Let's drink a toast to her.' He lifted his glass. 'Mother's Day!'

They all echoed the toast.

Having been handed the movie ball, Jake Freedman proceeded to run with it, giving her mother so much charming attention, Laura

couldn't help liking him for it. He was probably working hard at being an amenable guest,
showing off his talent for diplomacy to her
father. Nevertheless, it was giving her mother
pleasure, and her father, for once, was not sour-
ing it with any acid comments.

In fact, he looked surprisingly content with
the situation.

Laura didn't really care why.

It was good that he wasn't putting her mother
down as he usually did.

She slipped away to attend to the lunch prep-
arations, feeling slightly more at ease with Jake
Freedman's presence. It was making the day
run more smoothly than she had hoped for. The
only negative was his sexual impact on her.

She hadn't been able to stop herself from
slyly checking him over; the neat curl of his
ears, the length of his eyelashes, the sensuality of his lips, the charismatic flashes of his
smiles, the light sprinkle of black hairs on his

strong forearms, the elegant length of his fingers with their clean clipped nails, the way his muscular thighs stretched the black fabric of his jeans. And long feet! Didn't that mean his private parts would be…very manly?

Which, of course, would be in keeping with the rest of him.

It was all very difficult, knowing he was her father's man. It was also difficult to concentrate on getting everything right for the meal; vegetables to go into the oven, reheating the soup, greens ready for last-minute microwaving, mint sauce on the dining-room table. She would have to sit next to him again; probably a blessing since this table wasn't a round one and he couldn't see what was written on her face unless he turned to her.

So far, he wasn't giving her any special attention and it was probably better if it stayed that way—no dilemma between temptation and caution. He was bound to have a woman in the wings, anyway. Eddie had girls falling all over him and she couldn't imagine it would be any different for Jake Freedman—another reason for not getting involved with him. Being perceived as just one of an available crowd had no appeal.

Although being the boss's daughter, he would have to treat her with respect.

Which she'd hate.

Whatever way she looked at it, having Jake Freedman was no good. Besides, he wasn't exactly holding out the chance to have him, though he might before the day was over. As her mother said, there had to be a purpose behind this visit. If a connection with her was the desired end, she had to be ready for it, ready to say no.

The soup was hot enough to serve. Telling herself she was lucky to have the distraction of being the cook, Laura returned to the patio to invite everyone inside for lunch. Eddie escorted her mother to the dining room. Jake Freedman followed with her father, the two men obviously on congenial terms.

Another warning.

Her father must have once been charming to her mother or she wouldn't have married him. His true character could not have emerged until she was completely under his domination. If Jake Freedman was of like mind, thinking he had the right—the power—to rule others' lives as he saw fit, she wanted nothing to do with him.

Jake continued to get his bearings with the Costarella family over lunch. Eddie had dropped out of school and left home at sixteen, getting himself a job as a backroom boy in one of the television studios.

'One day you'll regret not going on with your education,' his father said balefully.

He shrugged. 'Accountancy was never going to suit me, Dad.'

'No. Head in the clouds. Just like your mother.'

The tone of disgust caused Alicia to flush. She was a more fragile person than her perfectly groomed image presented, very nervy and too anxious to please. He was recalling Laura's comment that her mother needed her when she leapt to Alicia's defence.

'Oh, I think Mum's totally grounded when it comes to her garden.'

'Garden…movies…' Costarella scoffed. 'Alicia has led both of you astray with her interests. I had high hopes for you, Laura. Top of your school in mathematics…'

'Well, I have high hopes for myself, Dad. Sorry I can't please both of us,' she said with a rueful smile.

'Gardening…' he jeered.

'Landscape architecture is a bit more than that, Dad.'

No hesitation in standing up for herself.

Costarella huffed. 'At least you can cook. I'll say that for you. Enjoying the meal, Jake?'

'Very much.' He shot an appreciative smile at Laura. 'Top chef standard. The soup was delicious and I've never tasted better lamb and baked potatoes.'

She laughed. 'Top chef recipes from a TV cooking show. All it takes is dedication to following the instructions. You could do it yourself if you had the will to. It's not a female prerogative. In fact, most of the top chefs are male. Do you cook for yourself?'

'No. Mostly I eat out.'

'Need a woman to cook for you,' Costarella slid in.

It was a totally sexist remark and he saw the recoil from it in Laura's eyes, followed by a derisive flash at him...if he thought the same.

He turned to Costarella and allowed himself one risky remark, grinning to take away any sting. 'Given that most top chefs are male, a man might be better.'

Eddie found this hilarious, cracking up with laughter.

'What's so funny?' his father demanded.

'It's just that lots of guys in the service industry are gay and I don't see Jake as gay,' he spluttered out.

Laura started giggling, too.

'I'm not,' Jake said.

'Certainly not,' Costarella declared emphatically.

'We know you're not,' Laura assured him, still tittering.

'Absolutely.' Eddie backed up. 'Laura wouldn't think you were sexy if you were gay.'

'Eddie, behave yourself,' Alicia cried.

'Impossible,' his father muttered, though his ill humour had dissipated at this affirmation that his daughter was vulnerable to the attraction he favoured.

Laura rose from the table. 'Now that you've embarrassed both of us, Eddie, I'm going to serve sweets, which I hope will be tart enough to glue up your mouth.' She smiled at her mother. 'It's lemon-lime, Mum.'

'Oh, my favourite!' Alicia glowed with pleasure. 'Thank you, dear.'

Jake watched her head off to the kitchen again. It would be risky business, taking on a connection with her, complicating what had been his undeviating purpose for too many years to mess with when he was in sight of the end. She could become a distraction. He'd been single-minded for so long, readjusting his thinking to include a relationship with Costarella's daughter was probably not a good idea, however tempting it was.

Cynically dating her for short-term benefits at work was no longer an option. He was genuinely attracted to her. Strongly attracted to her. She had his skin prickling with the desire for action between them. Costarella expected him to make a move on her. *He* wanted to make a move on her. The tricky part was controlling it.

'How come you're not sharing Mother's Day with your own Mum, Jake?' Eddie suddenly asked.

'I would be if she were still alive, Eddie,' he answered ruefully.

'Oh! Sorry!' He made an apologetic grimace. 'Hope the bereavement isn't recent.'

'No.'

'Guess I'm lucky I've still got mine.' He leaned over to plant a kiss on Alicia's cheek.

'Yes, since you've always been a mother's boy,' Costarella sniped.

There was a flicker of fear in the look Alicia darted at her husband. Jake imagined she had been a victim of abuse for so long, she felt helpless to do anything about it.

'I've been admiring the very artistic centre-piece for the table,' he said, smiling at her to take the anxiety away. 'Are they flowers from your garden, Alicia?'

'Yes.' Her face lit up with pleasure. 'I did that arrangement this morning. I'm very proud of my chrysanthemums.'

'And rightly so, Mum,' Laura chimed in, wheeling the traymobile into the dining room. 'They're blooming beautifully.'

She served the lemon-lime tart with dollops of cream to everyone, continuing her praise of her mother's talent for horticulture.

Jake watched her. She was beautiful. And smart. And so lushly sexy, temptation roared through him, defying the reservations that had been swimming through his mind.

As she resumed the seat beside him, he turned to her, his eyes seeking to engage hers with what he wanted. 'I'd like to see this garden. Will you show it to me when we've finished lunch?'

Startled, frightened, recoiling. 'Much better for Mum to show you, Jake. It's her creation.'

'He asked *you,* Laura,' Costarella immediately bored in. 'Not only should you oblige our guest, but your mother has already shown Eddie around the garden. She doesn't need to repeat herself, do you, Alicia?'

'No, no,' she agreed, her hands fluttering an appeal to her daughter. 'I'm happy for you to do it, Laura.'

Caught.

She had to do it now whether she wanted to or not.

Jake aimed at sweetening the deal for her. 'I'm interested in seeing it through your eyes. You can tell me how it fits your concept of landscape design.'

'Okay! I'll flood you with knowledge,' she said tartly.

He laughed. 'Thank you. I will enjoy that.'

Surrender under fire, Jake thought, but no surrender in her heart. It made for one hell of a challenge...their walk in the garden. The adrenaline charge inside him wanted to fight her reluctance to involve herself with him, yet that same reluctance gave him an out from Costarella's heavy-handed matchmaking... keeping the more important mission on track, without distraction.

He would make the decision later.

In the garden.

CHAPTER THREE

LAURA told herself it was just a job she had to take on and get through—escort Jake around the garden, bore him to death with her enthusiasm for built environments and deliver him back to her father, who had announced his intention to watch a football game on television in the home theatre.

Eddie helped clear the table, following her to the kitchen to have a private word with her as they stacked the dishwasher. 'You're the main target today, Laura. No doubt about it now,' he warned. 'I'd say Dad wants Jake as his son-in-law.'

'It's not going to happen,' she snapped.

'He's a clever guy. Been playing all sides

today. And I've been watching you. You're not immune to him.'

'Which made it very stupid of you to tell him what I thought.'

'Obvious anyway. Believe me, a guy like that knows women think he's sexy. He would have had them vying for his attention from his teens onwards. Just don't say yes to him.'

Easy for him, sitting on the sidelines, Laura thought savagely. 'What if I want to?'

Eddie looked appalled.

'He *is* sexy,' she repeated defiantly, fed up with being put on the spot.

He grimaced. 'Then make damned sure you keep it at sex and don't end up hooked on him. The way Mum is should be warning enough for you.'

'I will never be like Mum.'

He shook his head. 'I wish she would leave him.'

'She can't see anything else. Better play a

game of Scrabble with her while I'm doing my duty with Jake. She likes that.'

'Will do. That's a lot more fun than duty.'

Laura heaved a deep sigh, trying to relax the tension tearing at her nerves. 'I don't want to want him, Eddie.'

He gave her a look of serious consideration. 'Go for it if you must. You'll always wonder otherwise. Sooner or later he'll turn you off and I think you're strong enough to walk away.'

'Yes, I am,' she said with certainty.

'But you'd be better off not going there.'

'I know.' She made a rueful grimace. 'Maybe he'll turn me off out in the garden.'

'Unlikely.'

'Well I won't be falling at his feet, that's for sure. And you let Mum win at Scrabble, but don't be obvious about it.'

'No problem.' He grinned his devil-may-care grin. 'Let's go and fight the good fight.'

She grinned back at him. 'The *gay* bit was good.'

He laughed and hugged her shoulders as they returned to the dining room, where he immediately put their plan into action. 'Better get out the Scrabble, Mum. Since you beat me last time, I want a return match, and heaven help me if I'm swamped with all vowels again.'

'I'll leave you to your game,' her father said good-humouredly, rising from his chair, smiling at Jake Freedman. 'I'm sure you'll enjoy my daughter's company.'

'I will,' he agreed, rising to his feet, as well, ready to take on the garden seduction scenario.

Resentment suddenly raged through Laura. Jake Freedman was playing her father's game, but she didn't have to. He wasn't *her* guest. It was after three o'clock. Lunch had gone off reasonably well. The trickiest part of being together for Mother's Day was over. Her father was sparing them his presence. His wrath wouldn't fall on all of them if she didn't remain polite to the man. She could put Jake Freedman on the spot, instead of being the target herself.

She smiled at him. 'Let's go.'

He accompanied her outside, making easy conversation to start with.

'*Was* it your mother's pleasure in her garden that led you to your choice of career, Laura?'

He seemed genuinely curious and she didn't mind answering him. 'Partly. Nick probably had more influence, the creativity he uses to generate Mum's pleasure.'

'Who's Nick?'

'The gardener and handyman Dad employs to maintain everything, but he actually does more than maintain.'

'Like what?'

'He thinks about what will delight Mum and does it. Like the solar lights he's just put around the rockpool. I'll show you. It's over this way.'

He strolled beside her, apparently content to

bide his time, ensure she was relaxed with him. Which was totally impossible, but at least he didn't know it and wouldn't know it until he made a move on her.

'A waterfall, too,' he remarked as they came to the pool.

'Yes. It makes a soothing sound. Most people enjoy sitting near falling water…fountains in a park. Also reflections in water. The lights placed around the pool shimmer in it when it's dark.'

'Does your mother come out here at night?'

'Sometimes. Though she can also see this part of the garden from her bedroom window. What's really special is how Nick lit up the figurines of the Chinese water-carriers coming down the rocks at the side of the waterfall. There's another light at the back of the pot-plant below them. It bathes them in a ghostly glow. Quite a wonderful effect.'

'Landscape architecture,' he said, slanting

her a rueful smile. 'I've never thought about it but I can see why it should be appreciated.'

'I guess in the career you've chosen, you don't take the time to smell the roses,' she shot at him.

'True. I haven't,' he conceded readily enough, as though it didn't matter to him.

It niggled Laura into asking, 'Is it worth it?'

There was a subtle shift of expression on his face, a hardening of his jaw, a determined glint in his eyes. 'Yes, it is. To me,' he answered in a tone that didn't allow for a different point of view.

Laura couldn't leave it alone. 'You like working for my father?'

'Your father is part of a system that interests me.'

It was a clever sidestep, depersonalising her question.

'The system,' she repeated, wanting to nail

down his motivation. 'I can't imagine any pleasure in dealing with bankruptcy.'

'No, it can be very traumatic,' he said quietly. 'I would like to make it less so.' The dark brown eyes drilled into hers. 'Not even the most beautiful parks in the world resonate with people in that situation, Laura. All they see is their lives crumbling, their jobs gone, their plans for the future shattered. It can lead to divorce, suicide, violence, depression so dark there is no light.'

She shivered at the intensity of feeling coming from him, a depth of caring she hadn't expected in this man. It didn't sit with coldly calculated ambition. Not only that, but he'd also somehow turned the tables on her, making his job much more seriously special than hers.

'I know that people going through trauma do find some solace in a pleasant environment,' she argued with conviction. Her mother, for one.

'I didn't mean to undervalue it.' He gestured
an appeal. 'I'm not your father, Laura. Perhaps
we can both work on having open minds about
each other.'

'Why did you come here today?' she asked
point-blank.

'Your father wanted me to meet you and I
was curious enough to accept the invitation,'
he answered, his eyes gently mocking the hard
challenge in hers.

She planted her hands on her hips, sick of
how he was churning her around and wanting
open confrontation. 'So what do you think of
me?'

His mouth moved into a very sensual smile.
'I think you're *very* sexy.'

A tidal wave of heat rushed through Laura.
She snatched at his own words to her and threw
them back at him. 'That doesn't have much
currency with me.'

He laughed and stepped forward, sliding an

arm around her waist and scooping her into body contact with him, his eyes glittering with reckless intent. 'I've been wanting to do this from the moment we met, so I'll do it, and you can slap me down afterwards.'

There was time—a few seconds—for her to slam her hands against his shoulders and push away. His mouth didn't crash down on hers. It seemed to her he lowered his head in slow motion, moving his free hand to tilt her face upwards. She did nothing, waiting for the collision of the kiss, wanting it, wanting to know if it would be better than any other kiss a man had given her.

A weird exhilaration was buzzing through her at being held in his embrace, as though he was the right man for her, the perfect man—a sensation she'd never felt until now. Whether it was his intense maleness, his strength, his aggressive confidence, his sexy physique…

Laura couldn't pin it down, but curiosity held her totally captive.

His lips brushed over hers with surprising gentleness, tantalising her, exciting her with a sensuality she had not expected. She *did* move her hands to his shoulders, but not to push away, to touch, to feel, to slide around his neck and hold his head to hers. She liked the shape of it, liked the clean, bristly thickness of his short hair—no gel.

He started tasting her, little flicks of his tongue slipping seductively between her lips, and she responded with her own provocative probing, wanting to taste him, a pulsing primitive streak urging her to goad him into less control. It was as though he was testing how good she was for him, whether she would be worth pursuing beyond today, and everything female in her wanted to blow him out of his mind.

A wild exultation zinged through her when

he plunged into a far more passionate kiss. No more holding her face. Both arms were around her, pressing her into intimate contact with him and she revelled in the hard evidence of her desirability. He was very definitely aroused, and so was she, as fiercely passionate as he was in the meshing of their mouths, seeking and driving for more and more excitement.

He clutched her bottom, grinding her even closer, and she was so hot for him she didn't care how intimate they were. Her heart was pounding, her thighs were quivering, and the only thought she had was *yes, yes, yes*. It was powering through her. More than desire. Need that craved instant satisfaction. Urgently.

It was he who pulled back, breaking the kiss, lifting his head, sucking in air like a runner at the end of a marathon. She gulped in oxygen, too, the dizziness in her head demanding it. Her breasts were still crushed against his chest and she could feel his heart thumping in unison with hers. Then his cheek was rubbing against her hair and his voice vibrated in her ear.

'I want you, Laura, but it can't be here.'

Here…in the garden…in open view of anyone who wandered outside. Madness. She couldn't take him inside, either. Everyone would know. She recoiled from giving her father the satisfaction of thinking his plan was working. It would worry her mother. Eddie, too. It couldn't be done. The time and place wasn't right. But the man was. Which was very confusing because he shouldn't be.

'I need to sit down,' she said, acutely aware of how shaken she was. 'There's a garden bench…'

'I see it.'

He shifted, tucking her tightly against him, walking her to the bench. Laura had to concentrate on putting one foot in front of the other. He saw her seated then sat beside her, leaning forward, elbows on knees, still recovering himself from the rage of desire that had swept through both of them.

Laura breathed in the scent of the nearby lavender bush. It was supposed to be calming. It did help to clear her head to some extent. Jake Freedman might be his own man but he *was* closely connected to her father. However *right* he might feel to her, she couldn't overlook that situation.

'If you think this means I'm a pushover for the taking, it doesn't,' she blurted out. 'The chemistry between us is just chemistry and I won't be losing sight of that, so don't imagine it gives you any power over me.'

He nodded a few times, then shot her a wry smile. 'Well, you've certainly slapped me down.'

Not for the kiss. For the possible motive hidden behind it because the kiss had got to her, more powerfully than she cared to admit. She tore her gaze away from his tantalising little smile and stared at the waterfall, wishing it could soothe the deep disturbance this man had caused.

'Not so much a slap, Jake,' she said more calmly. 'Just letting you know how I feel about it. My father is obviously pushing me at you. Maybe he wants you as his son-in-law. No way will I be used as a step up your career ladder.'

No comment from him.

His silence went on for so long it began to shred her nerves. 'Sorry if I've dashed your hopes,' she said bitingly.

'Not at all.' He sat up, hooking his arms on the backrest of the bench in a totally relaxed manner, smiling at her as though he was perfectly at peace with her decision. 'I'm not looking for a wife at this point in my life and you're not looking to fill that position. With that understood, do you want any part of me, Laura?'

Which put her right back on the spot.

His eyes glittered with the knowledge that

she did, but wanting and taking were two different things. As Eddie said, she'd be better off not going there. Jake could be lying, secretly thinking he could seduce her into becoming his wife. Not that he'd be able to, but if she entered into any kind of relationship with him, he could report to her father that everything was sweet between them, and she'd hate that.

Yet looking at him, remembering how it had felt with him, the thought of not experiencing more of him actually hurt. Which was probably another danger signal. He *did* have power over her.

'I want you,' he said quietly, seeing her struggle with his question. 'Not because you're your father's daughter. I think the chemistry between us makes that totally irrelevant. I want you because I can't remember wanting any other woman quite as much.'

It echoed her response to him. Jake Freedman was definitely the ultimate ten out of ten. But he could be saying those words because they were what any woman would like to hear. He was such a sexy man, he might affect every woman this way and she was no exception at all to him. *Clever, playing all sides,* Eddie had said.

She eyed him sceptically. 'Is that the honest truth, Jake?'

'Much to my own dismay, yes,' he said with a rueful grimace.

It was an odd thing to say and she looked at him in puzzlement. 'Why to your dismay?'

The riveting brown eyes bored into hers with heart-stopping intensity. 'Because I don't want to want you, Laura. Any more than you want to want me. And with that said, why don't we both take time to think about it?'

He rose from the garden bench, apparently preparing to leave her. Laura was so startled by the action, she simply stared up at him.

'Do you have a mobile phone?' he asked.

'Yes.'

'Give me your number. I'll call you at the end of the week if I'm still thinking of you and you can then say yes or no.'

It was so abrupt, hard, cut and dried, and the turbulent feelings it set off inside her made it difficult to think. Time…yes…time to decide if she couldn't bear not to know more of him… or time to have his impact recede to something less significant.

He took a slim mobile phone out of his shirt pocket and she rattled out her number for him to enter it in his private file.

'Thank you,' he said, pocketing the phone again and flashing an ironic smile at her. 'I've seen enough of the garden. You might like to join Eddie and your mother playing Scrabble. I'll say goodbye to them and then to your father on my way out.'

Relief poured through her. No more stress today. Decision-making could wait. She returned his smile as she rose from the bench. 'I didn't have you pegged as a garden man.'

'I shall take up smelling roses.'

'You need a garden for that. The hothouse ones don't have much scent.'

He raised one eyebrow in a lightly mocking challenge. 'Perhaps we can give each other new experiences.'

She shrugged, deliberately noncommittal. 'Perhaps we can.'

No more was said.

He accompanied her back to the dining room and with every step she sensed him withdrawing from her, wrapping himself in self-containment. It was a weird, cold feeling—in sharp contrast to the wild heat of their physical connection. He was leaving her alone and that troubled her far more than it should.

Eddie and her mother said all the polite responses to his polite appreciation of the day spent with them. Her mother took him in tow to the lounge room so he could say goodbye to her father and she was left behind in the dining room with Eddie, whose eyes were full of questions.

'So?' he asked, as soon as their visitor was out of earshot.

'So, nothing,' she answered. 'I showed him the garden.'

She couldn't bring herself to open up a discussion on what had happened between her and Jake Freedman. Somehow it was too personal, too private.

Besides, it would probably come to nothing.

And it was probably better that way.

Probably.

CHAPTER FOUR

THE end of the week, he'd said.

It was the first thought Laura had when she woke up on Friday morning.

If he was still thinking of her, she mentally added, half-hoping that he wasn't so she wouldn't be faced with the decision of whether or not to see him again.

It had been impossible to get him out of her head. She couldn't look at a guy without comparing him to Jake Freedman. None of them measured up to him. Not even close. Her uni studies had suffered with him slipping into her mind when she should have been concentrating. As for being a Director of First Impressions at her receptionist job, no impressions at all had got through to her. Directing the doctors' patients had all been a matter of rote this week. It was like her whole life was revolving around waiting for his call.

Which was really, really bad.

What had happened to her strong sense of independence? It should be rising above this obsessive thinking about a man, putting him in a place of relative unimportance. She didn't like not being in full control of her life. It was as though a virus had invaded her system and she couldn't get rid of it. But as all viruses did, it would run its course and leave her, she told herself.

Especially if Jake didn't call.

However, if he did…

Laura heaved a fretful sigh and rolled out of bed, unable to make up her mind on what she should do. Would she always wonder about him if she didn't try him out?

It was an unanswerable question. Nevertheless, it plagued her all day, distracting her from the lectures at uni. By late afternoon she had decided it was best if Jake didn't call so a choice wasn't even available. She felt so woolly-headed, it was a relief to board the ferry from Circular Quay to Mosman and stand on the outside deck, needing a blast of sea breeze to whip away the fog in her mind.

The ferry was halfway across the harbour when her mobile phone rang. Her heart instantly started hammering. It might not be him, she told herself, plucking the phone out of the side pocket of her bag. He would not have finished work yet. It wasn't quite five o'clock. Her father rarely arrived home before seven.

Gingerly she raised the phone to her ear and said, 'Hello.'

'It's Jake, Laura.'

His voice conjured up his image so sharply, her breath stuck in her throat.

'Would you like to go out to dinner with me tomorrow night?'

Dinner! Her head whirled. To go or not to go…

'I thought we could try Neil Perry's Spice Temple. A new experience for both of us if you haven't been there.'

Neil Perry…one of Sydney's master chefs! His restaurants were famous for their wonderful food. The Rockpool. The Rockpool Bar and Grill. The Spice Temple. She would love, love, love to eat there, but…

'I can't afford it.'

'My treat. You gave me a great meal last Sunday.'

True. He owed her. 'Okay. I'd like that very much,' she said recklessly. A Neil Perry dinner was worth one evening with the man, regardless of what inner turmoil he caused. And maybe that would stop on further acquaintance. 'I'll meet you there,' she quickly added, not wanting her father to know she was seeing Jake Freedman again. 'What time?'

'Will seven o'clock suit?'

'Yes.'

'You know the address?'

'I'll look it up.'

'It's a basement restaurant. Go straight down-stairs. I'll wait for you inside.'

'I won't be late. Thanks for the invitation.'

She ended the call, quite pleased with herself for handling it with a fair amount of control. This meeting could be contained at the restaurant…if she wanted it to be. Eddie would let her stay over at his apartment in Paddington on Saturday night so being taken home by Jake could be avoided, too.

Excitement buzzed through her…wicked, wanton excitement.

A sexy man, a sexy meal…impossible not to look forward to experiencing both.

Jake steeled himself for the Friday afternoon wrap-up meeting in Alex Costarella's office,

suspecting there was only one issue of real interest on the agenda. He was right. After a half-
hour chat about the week's work, Costarella
leaned back in his executive chair, a smug little
man-to-man smile on his face as he asked,
'Will you be seeing Laura this weekend?'

'Yes. We're having dinner together tomorrow
night,' he answered, hating this matchmaking
farce, but knowing that going along with it
was to his advantage, keeping his position in
the company ripple-free until he was ready to
strike.

'Good! Good!'

Jake smiled back, playing the game to the
hilt. 'Thank you for introducing me to her.'

'Pleasure. Laura needs a man to take her in
hand and I hope you're the man to do it, Jake.'

The only way he was going to take her in
hand was in bed, if she agreed to it. 'She's
certainly very attractive.'

It was a noncommittal statement but Costarella

found it encouraging enough to let the matter pass. 'Enjoy your weekend,' he said, and Jake was free to leave.

He'd thought a lot about Laura Costarella since last Sunday. She was hostile to her father, hostile to his wishes, and he'd anticipated her saying no to the dinner invitation. Since he very much wanted her to say yes, he'd deliberately used the Neil Perry drawcard, knowing that her interest in cooking had to make her something of a foodie.

Temptation…

The stronger it was, the harder it was to resist.

She wanted him, too. No doubt about that. If she was up for a wild fling with him, Jake would be only too happy to oblige. He'd been itching to oblige all week. Satisfying the lust she'd triggered in him was fast becoming a must-do, though he did feel ambivalent about taking on Costarella's daughter. He hadn't counted on liking her and he certainly didn't want to begin caring about her.

Spicy company, spicy food, spicy sex.

That had to be the limit of his involvement with the daughter of his enemy because a line would be driven between them when he brought charges against her father, ensuring that the corrupt insolvency practitioner could never again bury another struggling business to secure his obscene liquidator's fee.

Lust always burned out after a while, he assured himself.

In the meantime, the fire had been lit for tomorrow night and he looked forward to some very spicy heat.

Laura stood in front of the billowing turquoise hologram that gave an exotic curtain illusion to the doorway leading to the Spice Temple. It should have added pleasure to her dressing up for this dinner date. She was wearing her sexiest dress—a short turquoise silk bubble skirt attached to a tightly fitting black silk bodice—and the gorgeous black-and-turquoise high heels her mother had bought her for Christmas. Nothing, however, could dispel the anger festering in her mind and churning through her stomach.

Jake Freedman deserved to be stood up. Only the lure of Neil Perry's food had brought her here and she *was* owed a dinner. As for her outfit, she hoped it made Jake Freedman want her all the more because he could eat his heart out for sex tonight. No way was he going to get as much as a piece of her.

'Have a nice night with Jake!'

Her teeth gnashed over those words—accompanied by her father's beaming smile of approval. He'd been told about this date. Maybe the two men had plotted it together. Whatever… Tonight was no longer a private and personal meeting. It reeked of other agendas in the wind and she hated the thought of playing a part in either man's scheming.

Determined on focusing on the food and giving Jake Freedman a very cold shoulder, she stepped past the doorway and made her way downstairs. Red dominated the decor of the basement restaurant. The scent of joss-sticks wafted through it. Definitely the hot, *in* place to be, Laura thought, noting that most of the tables were already occupied, even at this relatively early hour.

Jake had a table for two. He rose from his chair as he saw her being led to it, his gaze swiftly raking over the high points of her femininity, before shooting her a look of sizzling appreciation. Laura sizzled, too, not only with the acute, physical awareness he sparked off, but also with resentment at the sheer animal magnetism that clutched at her heart and turned her insides to jelly.

His clothes were completely nondescript—

white shirt, grey slacks. They were irrelevant to the stunning impact of the man, as though it was his natural right to hold centre stage anywhere, in any company without any effort whatsoever. He waited for her with easy confidence and Laura wished she could knock him down and sweep him out of her life as though his existence was of no account.

Somehow she had to make it of no account.

'You look spectacular,' he said in greeting, grinning wickedly as he added, 'Great shoes!'

'They're good man-stomping shoes,' she replied, doing her best to appear cool and collected.

One black eyebrow quirked upwards. 'About to do some stomping?'

She returned a glowering look. 'I'll eat first.'

'Good idea! Work up some energy.'

He was amused.

Laura seethed over his amusement as she sat down. They were handed menus by a waitress who offered to help them make choices if they wanted anything explained.

'Not yet,' Laura said firmly. 'I want to salivate over every dish before I start choosing.'

'We'll call you when we're ready,' Jake put in, smiling his charming smile, which, of course, would bring the dazzled waitress running the moment he caught her attention.

Laura fixed her attention on the menu. She read the Spice Temple philosophy first. It described what the restaurant aimed for—unique and special dishes, seasoned by an unmistakable Chinese flavour and driven by a long-fostered passion for Asian cuisine, all designed to delight the senses with their contrasting tastes and textures. She hoped they would dominate her senses and block Jake Freedman out.

'Why do you want to stomp on me?'

She set the menu down and glared at the curiosity in his eyes. 'How many brownie points did you get for telling my father we were meeting for dinner tonight?'

'Ah!' He made a rueful grimace. 'I didn't offer the information, Laura. He asked me directly if I was seeing you again. Did you want me to lie about it?'

She was unappeased. 'I bet you knew he would ask. That's why you called me when you did. Before you left work yesterday.'

He cocked his head on one side, the dark brown eyes challenging her stance on this issue. 'I thought you were determined on not having your father rule your life.'

'He doesn't.'

'He's influencing your attitude towards me right now.'

'Because you told him.'

He shook his head. 'You should make decisions for yourself, Laura, regardless of what anyone else knows or says. You made yours yesterday. Why let him change what you want?

You've brought him here with you instead of moving to your own beat.'

She frowned, realising she had let her father ruin all her pleasure in anticipating this date. Although how could she be excited over being used?

'What about you? Are you here for me or for him?' she asked, watching for any shiftiness in his eyes.

He grinned a wickedly sexy grin. 'When I was watching you walk to this table, I can assure you I was not thinking of your father.'

Heat bloomed in her cheeks at the provocative statement. She lifted her chin, defying the desire he wanted her to share. 'I decided to flaunt what you weren't going to get.'

'Decisions, decisions,' he mocked, gesturing an appeal. 'Can we leave your father out of them for the rest of this evening? Just enjoy all there is to enjoy just between ourselves?'

He was very appealing.

The man had everything—looks, intelligence, the sexiest eyes in the world, and he was undermining her prejudice at a rate of knots. Nevertheless, she couldn't quite set aside an ulterior motive for this date with her. On the other hand, why shouldn't she take pleasure in being with him, move her father to the sidelines, denying him any power to influence the play between her and Jake? After all, she was the one with the power to decide how far she would get involved with this man.

She gave him a hard look of warning. 'As long as it's kept between ourselves, I'm happy to take a more positive attitude towards you.'

'And I'm happy to be your secret lover,' he replied, his eyes dancing with unholy teasing.

Her heart performed a somersault. 'I didn't say anything about becoming lovers.'

'Just assuring you that private moments will be kept private.' He opened up his menu. 'Let's salivate over what's on offer together. Did you see that the hottest dishes are printed in red?'

He was the hottest dish.

Laura dragged her mind off visualising him as her lover and reopened her menu. 'I prefer spicy to hot, hot,' she said, looking at the list of entrées.

'Okay. We cross out the red print ones.'

'You don't have to. Choose whatever you like.'

'There's so much to like, it will be better if we can share, don't you think? Have a taste of each other's choices? Broaden the experience?'

Sharing the taste… Laura's stomach curled. It sounded intimate. It was intimate. And suddenly she didn't care about other agendas. She wanted this experience with him.

'Great idea!' she said, and allowed herself to smile.

His eyes twinkled with pleasure, completely

dissipating the anger she had carried to this meeting.

'You're incredibly beautiful when you smile,' he remarked. 'I hope I can make you smile all evening for the sheer pleasure of looking at you.'

She laughed. 'No chance! I'm going to be busy eating.'

'I'll try for in between bites.'

'I'll be drooling over the food.'

He laughed. 'Speaking of which, what entrées would you like to try?'

A smile was still on her face as she read the yummy list. The happy excitement about tonight with Jake had come bouncing back. He was right about making decisions for herself. She should trust her own instincts and go with what instinctively felt right.

CHAPTER FIVE

THE waitress advised them to choose only one main course with a side dish of vegetables to share since they were ordering two separate entrées. The helpings were large and they would surely want to leave room for dessert.

'Definitely,' Laura agreed. 'I have to try the sesame ice cream with candied popcorn and chocolate.'

'And I want the Dessert Cocktail,' Jake said with relish. 'Sounds wonderful—caramelized pear, London gin, lillet blanc and crème de cacao shaken and served with the chocolate, sesame and cashew bark.'

It sounded very James Bond to Laura who couldn't help grinning over the thought. Jake might not be 007 but he was certainly tall, dark, handsome and dangerous, especially to any peace of mind. Somehow peace of mind wasn't rating highly at the moment. A thrilling buzz was running through her veins and she was now determined on milking maximum enjoyment out of the night, throwing caution and the Machiavellian shadow of her father to the winds.

'That's a big smile,' Jake commented, his eyes simmering sexily.

'Loving the idea of having a piece of your dessert,' she tossed back, knowing she wanted a piece of him, too.

'Food, glorious food!' he quoted from the musical *Oliver*, half singing the words and making her laugh.

'We have to decide on which one of our main courses to go for now,' she reminded him.

'We'll go with your choice—the stir-fried pork, bacon, smoked tofu, garlic shoots, garlic

chives and chilli oil—and I'll pick the veg-
etable dish.'

'Which will be?'

'Stir-fried wild bamboo pith, snow peas and
quail eggs with ginger and garlic.'

'We'll probably end up with garlic breath.'

'We can try washing it away with wine.'

He ordered an expensive bottle of sauvignon
blanc.

The waitress departed, having assured them
of prompt service.

Laura heaved a satisfied sigh as she sat back
and relaxed, happy to enjoy the ambience of
the restaurant and the company of the man she
was with.

'How was your week?' she asked.

He gave her a very sensual smile. 'All the
better for ending here with you. How was
yours?'

'Annoying.'

He raised a quizzical eyebrow.

She made a rueful grimace. 'I couldn't get you out of my head.'

He laughed. 'I'm glad the problem wasn't entirely mine. The question is whether to feed the fever or starve it?'

'I'm all for feeding tonight.'

'So am I.'

His eyes said he wanted to eat her all up and Laura couldn't deny she wanted to taste him again, too, but she wasn't ready to commit herself to becoming lovers on such short acquaintance.

'I meant here at the restaurant, Jake. I don't really know you, do I?' She eyed him seriously. 'My father obviously likes you very much, which isn't a great recommendation. I think from your visit last Sunday, you can draw a fairly clear picture of my life, but I don't have one of yours, apart from your mentioning that your mother has passed away. What about the rest of your family?

He shrugged. 'Both my parents died when I was eighteen. I was their only child. I've been on my own ever since. My life is not complicated by having to manage relationships, Laura. As I saw you doing last Sunday.'

'You move to your own beat,' she said wryly.

'Yes.'

'No live-in girlfriends along the way to here and now?'

He shook his head. 'I haven't met anyone I wanted to be with every day.'

She nodded, extremely wary of the live-in situation herself. 'It's a big ask, day in, day out. I can't see myself even wanting to try it.'

He smiled, eyes twinkling with understanding. 'You wish to be a free spirit.'

'I've seen my mother compromise too much,' she shot at him.

'Not all men are like your father, Laura,' he said seriously. 'My parents' marriage was very happy. I grew up in a loving home. I wish I still had it.'

She felt a stab of envy, though his loss triggered sympathy, as well. 'You were lucky to have what you did, Jake, but I guess missing that home life leaves you feeling very lonely.'

His eyelids dropped to half-mast, narrowing the flash of dangerous glitter. Some powerful emotion was coursing through him, belied by the offhand tone he used in his reply. 'It's been ten years, Laura. I've learnt to live with being alone.'

She didn't think so. She sensed anger in him at the loss, a deep abiding anger, so intense there was an edge of savagery to it. The image of a lone wolf endlessly prowling for some measure of satisfaction leapt into her mind.

Had he been looking for it in the career he had chosen? The bankruptcy business was centred on loss and he'd spoken almost passionately about the trauma of it and wanting to help when she'd taken him out to the garden last week. It had surprised her at the time. The conviction started to grow in her that he was not like her father. Not at all like him.

Which made the pleasure she could share with him much more acceptable.

'The self-sufficient man,' she said, smiling.

'Who doesn't want to be alone tonight.'

His smile was definitely wolfish, exciting her with the wild thought of howling at the moon together, mating on top of a mountain under the stars. Ridiculous since they were in the middle of a city, but the female animal inside her was strongly aroused, wanting to explore intimate possibilities with Jake Freedman.

The waitress returned with the bottle of wine and filled their glasses for them. Jake lifted his in a toast. 'To learning a lot more about each other.'

Laura nodded agreement. 'I'll drink to that.'

She clicked her glass to his and they both sipped the wine.

'I heard you tell Eddie that you worked out at a gym. Do you go often?'

'Usually after work. It's a good way of winding down.'

And every woman in the place would be eyeing him off, Laura thought, wondering if he also used the gym for casual pick-ups. She couldn't imagine him not having a very active sex life. Which, she strongly suspected, he kept completely separate from his work life.

'You said last Sunday you didn't want to want me, Jake,' she reminded him. 'Is that because it's difficult to avoid it touching on your career with me being my father's daughter?'

He made an ironic grimace. 'I think it's a complication we'd both prefer not to have.' He leaned forward, his dark riveting eyes shooting a blaze of purpose at her. 'Let's shut the door on it. Just do what we want to do together, regardless of other issues. Are you brave enough to go down that road with me, Laura? Strong enough to make the choice for yourself?'

The challenge propelled her pulse into overdrive. Brave? Strong? She wanted to belief that of herself, but was it really true? She'd always shied clear of intimate entanglements, afraid of how they might affect her. The couple of sexual experiments she'd allowed herself had been more out of curiosity—a desire for knowledge—than a wish for a closer, more possessive attachment.

Jake Freedman tapped something far more primal in her and that was scary because it was uncontrollable. She wanted to explore it, to feel whatever he could make her feel, but she couldn't quite override the sense of danger with him. Already he had taken up far too much possession of her mind. Would that go away with passion spent or would she end up losing the mental independence she needed for self-survival?

She could not—would not—end up like her mother.

'I like to come and go as I please, Jake,' she said firmly. 'I don't think I'd mind joining you along the road now and then, but…'

Her mouth dried up as a dazzling grin spread across his wickedly handsome face.

'Fine…perfect…we can draw a map and meet when the time is right for both of us.'

She laughed with nervous excitement. He was so obliging, so tempting, so incredibly sexy, and surely there was nothing too scary about having an intermittent adventure with him.

The waitress arrived with their entrées. Laura had chosen the fried salt-and-pepper silken tofu with spicy coriander salad and Jake had decided on the Northern-style lamb and fennel dumplings. Both dishes looked and smelled deliciously enticing.

'We divide them in half. Right?' she said eagerly.

'Sharing is the deal,' he agreed, obviously enjoying her keen anticipation. 'Go ahead. Divvy up.'

Jake watched her halve the portions on each plate, liking her meticulous care, liking everything about her, especially the determination to run her own life as she saw fit. It freed him of any guilt over pursuing what he wanted with her. She was not looking for a happy-ever-love with him. She didn't believe in it.

Given what he'd seen of her parents' marriage, he understood where she was coming from and why she would shy clear of serious attachments. Alex Costarella had wrought damage on his own family, as well as on many others'. He'd robbed Jake of his parents, but unlike them, Laura was alive and kicking. She would survive. An intermittent relationship with him should not create a problem for either of them.

'We should start with the dumplings and finish with the salad,' she said authoritatively.

'Yes, ma'am.'

It startled her into a laugh. 'I didn't mean to be bossy.'

He grinned. 'I don't mind taking advice from a serious foodie. In fact, I would like you to extend my education on gourmet delights.'

She blushed. 'You're teasing me. I think I'll just shut up and eat.'

'Enjoy.'

She ate with obvious relish. It was a pleasure watching her appreciating each different taste. 'Please feel free to comment,' he urged. 'I wasn't really teasing you, Laura. I want you to share your thoughts on these dishes with me.'

'Tell me what *you* think,' she countered.

He did and she happily responded.

The whole meal was a pleasure, not only for the wonderful variety of tastes, but also Laura's delight in them. She made it a great sensory experience and not only on the palate. The licking of her lips, the heavenly rolling of her eyes, the rise and fall of her lush breasts when she sighed with satisfaction, the warm smiles that fuelled a burning lust to have all of her…Jake itched to sweep her off to bed and take his fill of Laura Costarella.

He couldn't recall ever having enjoyed an evening with a woman so much. It was impossible to tolerate the thought of it ending here. He had to persuade her to want what he wanted. And not just tonight. He knew one night wouldn't satisfy him. Not now.

They finished up with nougatine and rum truffle candy bars to nibble as they sipped the last of the German Riesling he'd ordered to accompany their dessert.

'This has been fantastic, Jake. Thank you so

much for giving me the experience.' Her beautiful blue eyes twinkled. 'Definitely a more than fair exchange for my Sunday lunch.'

'Apart from Neil Perry, what other top Sydney chefs would you like to try out?' he asked, determined on tempting her into his company again.

She reeled off a number of names, then shook her head. 'I can't afford to go to their restaurants but one day I hope to. In the meantime, I drool over their cook books.'

'I can afford them, Laura, but I don't want to go alone. Nor do I know as much about food as you do. I'm happy to pay for you to be my educator, my companion, to share your knowledge and pleasure with me. Will you do that?'

She hesitated, frowning over his proposition.

'An adventure into fine dining,' he pressed.

'With you footing the bill,' she said, wincing over the inevitable cost.

'Why not? It's my idea.' Not to mention the desire running hot behind it.

'It's like…you're buying me, Jake.'

He shook his head. 'Buying your interest, your knowledge. Expanding my own. Say yes, Laura. It will be fun together. As tonight has been.'

Which was undeniable.

'You're right,' she said on a sigh of surrender. 'It's no fun alone. I'm sorry I can't pay my way but I simply don't earn enough with only a part-time job.'

He waved a dismissive hand. 'Don't worry about it. I'll consider it an investment in broadening my life.' He flashed her a mischievous grin. 'You could bring a garden rose for me to smell at our next restaurant. You're right about the hothouse ones sold by street vendors. They have no scent.'

She laughed, a lovely ripple of sound that was

headier than the wine. 'You actually went out and tried them?'

'I did.'

'Well, there's hope for you yet.'

'Hope for what?'

'For being more aware of nature's beautiful gifts.'

'I'm very aware of one sitting directly opposite me.' He reached across the table and took one of her hands in his, lightly rubbing his thumb over its palm as his eyes bored into hers, every forceful atom of his mind willing her to concede to the strong sexual attraction between them. 'Spend the night with me, Laura. I've booked a room in the Intercontinental Hotel. It's only a short walk from here. Let's satisfy what was left unsatisfied last Sunday.'

It was blunt.

It was honest.

It promised nothing more than it said.

It had to be this way or no way.

Despite all he liked about her, she was still Alex Costarella's daughter and that fact would separate them when the time for retribution came. Jake had been moving towards that destination for ten years. Whatever he had with Laura could only be a brief sidetrack.

CHAPTER SIX

A WILD MÊLÉE of emotions pumped through Laura's heart. The response of her body to Jake's proposition was instantaneous; her stomach contracting in sheer yearning for the satisfaction he promised, her thighs pressing together to contain the rush of excitement at their apex, her breasts tingling with the need to be touched, held, given the same sensual caressing he was using on her hand.

The simple answer was yes.

She wanted to go with him, wanted to feel how it would be, wanted to know, but the surge of desire was so compelling it frightened her. This wasn't just curiosity. Nor was it an experiment over which she had control.

And there were other considerations.

She was supposed to be spending the night at Eddie's apartment. Her brother would worry if she didn't turn up there so he would have to be told, though she need not actually speak to him. A text message would suffice. Eddie would undoubtedly repeat what he'd said before—*make damned sure you keep it at sex and don't get hooked on him.*

Good advice. Except Laura had the fluttery feeling that she was hooked. Deeply and irrevocably hooked. Although if Jake ever demanded too much of her, surely she had enough backbone to walk away. He was offering her great dinners and very probably great sex. It shouldn't be a problem for her to take both and enjoy both.

His thumb pressed into her palm. 'What reservations do you have, Laura?' he asked quietly, the dark brilliant eyes scouring hers for answers, challenging whatever barriers were in her mind.

Pride wouldn't allow her to admit she was scared of his power over her. It suddenly seemed terribly important to appear brave and strong, not only to him but also to herself. She forced a smile. 'None. I was just thinking I don't want to be left wondering, so let's do it.'

He relaxed into a laugh—a deep rumble of pleasure that thrummed along her shaky nerves, promising all would be well between them. His eyes sparkled delight in her as he said, 'You are one amazing woman.'

She raised her eyebrows in arch surprise. 'Why?'

He grinned. 'Before I met you I was expecting a pampered princess or a calculating miss, used to getting to her own way. It was a surprise to find you were neither. But you are quite strikingly beautiful, Laura, and beautiful women tend to use that power to see how far a man will go for them.'

'I don't like power games,' she said sharply, hating any form of manipulation.

'No. You're wonderfully direct with what you think.' He lifted his glass in a toast to her. 'May you always be so.'

She cocked her head on one side consideringly. 'Were you buttering me up with the foodie thing?'

He shook his head. 'I want more than a one-night stand with you. I'm quite certain I'll enjoy our adventure into fine dining.'

'So will I.'

'Then we're agreed on our points of contact.'

She laughed, happily giddy with the sense that this wasn't so much a dangerous trap she might fall into but a course of action that could give her tremendous pleasure. Her whole body zinged with excitement at the points of contact soon to be made.

'Will you excuse me for a few minutes?' she

said, rising from her chair. 'I need to go to the ladies' and call my brother.'

'Why your brother?' he asked, frowning over the possibility of third-party interference.

'I arranged to stay overnight at his apartment. I don't want Eddie worrying about me.'

'Ah! Of course! You didn't want your father to know. He won't know any more from me, Laura,' he quickly assured her.

She paused a moment, eyeing him with deadly seriousness. 'If you don't keep to that, Jake, I won't see you again.'

'Understood.'

A secret affair, Laura thought, liking the idea of it as she made her way to the ladies' room. Somehow it was less threatening than a relationship she would be expected to talk about. Eddie would have to know but she could trust him to keep it private if she asked him to. They had a solid sister/brother pact about running their own lives—away from their father.

However, she had no sooner sent the necessary text than her mobile phone rang in response. With a rueful sigh, she reopened it,
knowing Eddie was going to express concern.

'You said you weren't going to fall at his feet,'
he snapped in disapproval.

'I'm standing upright and walking to where
I want to go. Just like you do, Eddie,' she reminded him.

'You're younger than I am, Laura. Not as
street-hard. I tell you, that guy knows how to
play all the angles. You should be standing
back a bit, more on guard.'

She knew it was Jake's connection to her
father making her brother overprotective but
she had dealt with that issue. Until it raised its
head again—if it did—she was determined on
ignoring it and pleasing herself. 'I want this,
Eddie. Let it be. Okay?'

In the short silence that followed she had a
mental image of him grinding his teeth over

her decision, not liking it one bit but forced to respect it. 'Okay,' he said grudgingly. 'Will I see you tomorrow?'

'If you're at the apartment when I come to pick up the things I've left there.'

'I'll be in. Hope this isn't one hell of a mistake, Laura.'

'I hope so, too. 'Bye for now.'

She stared at her reflection in the mirror as she refreshed her lipstick. Her eyes were very bright. Feverishly bright? Earlier this week she had likened Jake to a virus that had invaded her system, knocking her out of kilter. The invasion was much stronger tonight, both physically and mentally, and she didn't want to fight it. Surrendering to all the clamouring feelings inside her had to be right. By tomorrow she would know for certain if it was a mistake. That was better than wondering.

Jake rose from his chair as she approached

their table again. 'Ready to go?' he asked as she reached it.

'Yes. Have you paid…?'

He nodded. 'And tipped. The service was excellent.'

'Absolutely. We didn't have to wait too long for anything.'

He smiled, the sexy simmer back in his eyes as he hooked her arm around his, drawing her into close physical contact with him and intimately murmuring, 'I'm glad you don't like waiting.'

Her ear tingled from the warm waft of his breath. Her heart leapt into a wild hammering as the thought jagged through her mind that she was being too easy for him—not waiting, plunging headlong into bed with him. Probably all women were *easy* for him and she would be no different to any of the others. But did that really matter? Wasn't she going after what *she* wanted? She didn't have to be different. She just had to be true to herself.

She sucked in a deep breath to calm herself as they moved towards the exit. 'I daresay you don't have to wait for much, Jake,' she said drily.

'You're wrong.' He slid her an ironic look. 'Some things I've been waiting years for.'

'Like what?'

She caught a savage glitter in his eyes before he turned his head away and shrugged. 'Just personal goals, Laura. I guess you're impatient to make a start on your career, but you have to wait until you get your degree under your belt.'

'It will be good to finally strike out on my own,' she agreed, wondering what his personal goals were and why they sparked such a flow of strong feeling in him. A dangerous man, she thought again, dangerous and driven, but driven by what?

'I'm sure you'll find your work-life very rewarding, caring about the environment as you do,' he remarked, sliding straight back into an admiring expression, shutting the door on what he obviously wanted to keep private.

Laura decided not to try probing. Later in the night when his guard was down and he was more relaxed, he might reveal more about himself. It could wait. Or maybe his goals were connected to her father. In which case, she didn't want to know. Not tonight. Tonight was about exploring something else entirely and she didn't want anything to spoil it.

As they emerged onto the street she hugged his arm, secretly revelling in its strongly muscled masculinity. Her imagination conjured up images of him naked—the perfect male in every respect. Every woman should be allowed to have one, she told herself, and this was simply seizing the opportunity. This connection to Jake Freedman didn't have to get complicated. In fact, she shouldn't let it

EMMA DARCY

117

become complicated. It was much safer to keep it simple.

'The hotel is about three blocks away,' he said, his mouth moving very sensually into a teasing little smile. 'Can you manage to walk that far in those gloriously erotic shoes or shall I flag down a taxi?'

She laughed, giddy with the thought of his mouth moving erotically all over her. 'I can walk, as long as it's a stroll and not a forced march.'

'I wouldn't force anything with you, Laura. This is all about choice,' he said seriously.

It was nice to have that assurance, to know she wasn't at physical risk with him. Strangely enough, it hadn't even occurred to her that she might be. It was the emotional risk she'd been concerned about. No man had ever affected her as Jake did.

'Why choose a hotel?' she asked as they

walked towards it. 'We could have gone to your place.'

'My place is barely habitable. It's an old run-down terrace house that I'm in the process of renovating. There's stuff everywhere. I hope I can make it look great when it's finished, but that's not tonight or any night soon. I only have time to work on it at weekends.'

'You're doing the renovating yourself?'

'Not all of it. Only the carpentry. My father taught me all the skills of the trade and I'm enjoying doing the work myself.'

'Your father was a carpenter?'

'No, he was an engineer but he loved working with wood. It was a hobby he shared with me in my growing-up years.'

The tone of deep affection told her he'd shared a very special bond with his father while Eddie had only ever known criticism and disapproval from their father and she had learnt to avoid the kind of contact that inevitably led to acrimony. Such different lives…

Possibly working with wood kept the family bond alive for Jake, though he'd also said last Sunday he liked to relax by doing something physical. Going to the gym was not his only outlet, and she liked the idea of him being involved with something creative. Renovating a house was similar to building an environment to a pre-designed plan.

Jake worked for her father but he definitely wasn't like him.

She would tell Eddie so tomorrow.

In the meantime, she couldn't resist lifting her free hand to slide her fingers across Jake's. 'Your skin isn't rough,' she remarked.

He was amused by her checking. 'I wear gloves for heavy work. You must do, too.' He caught her hand and held it, caressing it as he had before, smiling into her eyes. 'Definitely no calluses.'

Laura had difficulty catching her breath he was so utterly gorgeous and her mind was spinning with the wonder of how excited he made her feel. Only belatedly did it click into the line of conversation and produce a reply, the words coming out huskily. 'My mother's training. A lady should always protect her skin from damage.'

He stopped walking, halting both of them as he released her hand to lift his to her cheek, stroking it with exquisite softness. 'No damage,' he murmured.

His thumb slid under her chin, tilting it up. He unhooked his arm from hers and wrapped it around her waist. His head bent and Laura watched his mouth coming closer and closer, her heart hammering in wild anticipation for the kiss she had been remembering all week.

It didn't matter that they were standing on a public sidewalk in the centre of the city with people passing by. Everything beyond this moment with Jake faded into insignificance. The desire, the need to feel what he'd made her feel before, was pulsing through her.

His lips grazed over hers, igniting a host of electric tingles. His tongue flicked over them, soothing, seductively seeking entry, which she eagerly gave, wanting the deeper sensations, the erotic tasting, the rise of feverish passion that would blow away any lingering doubt about choosing to have this night with him.

Eagerly she surrendered her mouth to the intimate connection with his and almost instantly her inner excitement escalated, wiping all thought from her mind, making her super-aware of physical contact with him, the delicious pressure of touching points; breasts, stomach, thighs, a wild vibrancy pouring through her, making her ache with the intensity of feelings that had never been so overwhelmingly aroused.

This kiss was not just a kiss. It was total invasion, possession, wildfire sweeping beyond any control, burning her up with the need to have all of this man. Laura lost all sense of self. She was completely consumed by her response to him, and the response was too immediate, too powerful, too real for her to reason it away.

She wanted him.

More fiercely than she'd ever wanted anything.

It was a dizzying shock when he tore his mouth from hers and pressed her head onto his shoulder, making the separation decisive. Her heart was pumping so hard, the drumming of it filled her ears. Only vaguely did she hear him suck in breath. His chest expanded with it. He rubbed her back, probably an instinctive calming action. Her quivering nerve ends were grateful for it.

'Shouldn't have done that but I've been wanting to all evening,' he muttered. 'Are you okay to walk on, Laura?'

Hotel…alone together in private…bed…un-interrupted intimacy… 'Yes,' she breathed on a sigh that relieved some of the tense ache in her chest. 'As long as you hold on to me.'

A deep sexy laugh rumbled from his throat. 'Letting you go will be the problem, not hold-ing on to you.'

His words struck a vulnerable chord in her that Laura instantly shied away from examin-ing. 'Let's not think about problems,' she said quickly, lifting her head to shoot him a look of needful appeal. 'I only want to think about what we can have together.'

'So do I,' he answered, tenderly cupping her cheek as though she was something very precious, his dark eyes shining with pleasure in her. 'It's not far to the hotel now.'

'Okay. Give me your arm.'

He tucked her close to him. The shakiness in Laura's legs gradually lessened as they walked the rest of the way to the Intercontinental.

Neither of them spoke. They moved in a haze of mutual desire, impatient for the fulfilment of it, everything else irrelevant.

The hotel had been built around the old treasury building, making spectacular use of its special features. Laura had shared an afternoon tea with her mother there after a shopping day in the city. The main gathering place was The Cortile, a marvellous two-storeyed area covered by a huge glass dome, with colonnaded walkways surrounding it. Tonight, as Laura and Jake headed around it to the reception area, elegantly dressed people were indulging in a late supper, enjoying the ambience and the music being played on a grand piano.

It was a classy hotel and Laura couldn't help feeling pleased that Jake had chosen it. Somehow it made tonight with him more special. He collected their door-key from the receptionist and as they moved to the bank of elevators, he murmured, 'I took a Bayview room. It overlooks the Botanical Gardens. I thought you'd enjoy the view over breakfast.'

Laura's heart swelled with happiness. He'd been thinking of her, planning to give her pleasure. This wasn't just about sex with him. They were going to share more. Much more. She had made the right decision. A journey with Jake Freedman was well worth having. She no longer cared about how far it might go or where it might end. He was the man she wanted to be with.

CHAPTER SEVEN

J AKE quickly slid the door-key into the slot just inside the room and the lights came on. Everything looked fine—classy, welcoming, and most important of all, providing a private oasis, not touching on Laura's home environment nor his, completely separate to the lives they normally lived.

It had to be this way.

Bad enough that he was in the grip of uncontrollable desire for Alex Costarella's daughter. Boundaries to this affair had to be set and kept. He couldn't allow it to take over too much of his life. But right here and now he could satisfy his hunger for her, and to his immense relief she was up for it, no further delay to what they both wanted.

She walked ahead of him, moving towards the window seat with the view on the far side of the room. He watched the provocative sway of her hips, felt the tightening in his groin, started unbuttoning his shirt, impatient for action. She set her handbag on the desk as she passed it. Jake tossed his shirt on the chair in front of it, took off his shoes, his gaze fastening on her turquoise high heels with their seductive ankle straps. She had great legs and the thought of having them wound around him brought his erection to full tilt.

'Lots of city lights but it's too dark to see the botanical gardens,' she remarked.

'Won't be dark in the morning,' he muttered, unzipping his trousers.

She glanced back over her shoulder. 'I think I like this view better,' she said with sparkling interest, her eyes feasting on his bare chest and shoulders. 'I've been wondering how you'd look naked.'

He laughed, exhilarated by the honesty of her lust for him. He whipped off the rest of his clothes, dumping them on the chair with his shirt. 'Hope you're not disappointed,' he said, grinning with confidence, knowing his physique invariably drew attention from women at the gym.

'Not one bit,' she answered emphatically, examining all his *bits*, which raised the already high level of Jake's excitement.

She lifted an arm and hooked the long tumbling fall of her black curls away from her neck, her other hand reaching for the top of the zipper at the back of her dress, obviously intent on removing her own clothes.

'Let me,' Jake said hastily, finding the bared nape of her neck incredibly erotic and wanting the pleasure of slowly uncovering the rest of her, visually feasting on her lush femininity.

A few quick strides and he was taking over the task, opening up the snugly fitting bodice, exposing the satin-smooth, elegant slope of her back, which, delightfully, was uninterrupted by a bra. The line of her spine created an intriguing little valley that compelled his finger to stroke the lovely length of it. His touch raised a convulsive shiver of pleasure and he smiled, knowing her body was as taut with excitement as his own, every nerve alive with sensitivity.

Eager to see more of her, he unzipped the top of the skirt and peeled it from her hips, letting it fall to the floor. The sight of a sexy black G-string encircling her small waist and bisecting a totally luscious bottom sucked the air from his lungs and blistered his mind with urgent desire. He barely stopped himself from moving forward and fitting himself to the tantalising cleft.

Better to remove the last scrap of clothing first. He hooked his thumbs under the waistband and glided it over the soft mounds, down the long, lissom thighs and the taut curves of her calves, every millimetre raising the raging heat in his blood. The flimsy fabric caught on the straps of the erotic shoes. Couldn't leave them on. The stiletto heels could do him a damage in the throes of passion and Jake was already envisaging a huge amount of fantastic activity in bed.

'Sit down, Laura. Makes it easier to take your shoes off.'

He was still crouched, ready to free her feet when she swivelled around and sat on the window seat. The eye-level view of her beautiful full breasts was a mind-blowing distraction. She leaned back so they tilted up at him, large rosy aureoles with peaked nipples shooting temptation. He stared, captivated for several moments before gaining his wits to lift his gaze to see if she was deliberately teasing him.

Her thickly lashed blue eyes looked darker than before, simmering with an inviting sultriness. She wanted him enthralled by her fabulous femininity, wanted to drive him wild for her. Whether it was a deliberate exertion of her woman-power or not, it reminded Jake of who she was and how careful he had to be not to become ensnared by this woman.

He fixed his attention on the shoes, forced his fingers to undo the ankle straps. In a few moments he could take all he wanted of her, revel in having it, and he would, all night long, but come the morning he had to be sane enough to walk away from her and keep her at a mental distance until the next time they were together.

Shoes off.

They were both completely naked now.

He stood up, and the act of towering over her triggered his sense of man-power. He was in charge of this encounter. He'd brought her to this cave and he would control everything that happened between them. With a surge of adrenalin-pumped confidence he leaned over, gripped her waist and lifted her off the window-seat, whirling her straight over to the bed, laying her down, positioning himself beside her with one leg flung over hers, holding her captive so he could touch the rest of her at will.

'Kiss me again,' she commanded, her voice huskily inviting, her eyes glittering with the need for passion to blow them both away.

'I will,' he promised, but not her mouth, not yet.

The rose-red nipples were pointed up at him, hard evidence of her arousal and he wanted her more aroused than he was. He closed his mouth around them, drawing on the distended flesh, sucking, his tongue swirling, lashing. She wrapped her hands around his head, fingers thrusting through his hair, dragging on his scalp, her body arching, aching for a more consuming possession.

Not yet… Not yet…

He swept a trail of hot kisses down over her stomach to the arrow of dark springy curls leading to the most intimate cleft between her thighs. He could smell the wonderfully heady scent of her desire for him as he dipped his mouth into the soft folds of her sex, intent on driving this centre of excitement to fever pitch. He exulted in tasting her hot wetness, exulted even more as she writhed to the rhythm of his stroking, crying out at the frantic tension building up inside her, jack knifing up to grab his shoulders and tug his body over hers.

He was ready to oblige now, knowing her entire being was screaming for him and he was still in control, though bursting to unleash his own knife-edge desire. As he lifted himself up, her legs locked around him, her hips already rocking, and there was no more waiting. He surged into the slick passage to the edge of her womb and dropped his head to ravish her mouth, wanting total invasion, absolute domination of this intimate togetherness.

Yet she met the attack of his kiss with an assault of her own, a fusion of heat that turned aggression into a melting pot of exploding sensations and he lost every vestige of control. Her legs goaded him into a series of fast thrusts, clamping around him at the point of deepest penetration as she moaned at the intense satisfaction of it, then rolling her hips around the hard heated fullness of him as he withdrew to plunge again, driven to hear and feel her pleasure in him over and over, wildly intoxicated by the sense of being drawn from peak to peak, each one raising the stakes to a higher level of fierce feeling.

It was like riding a storm, hurtling towards the eye of it at breakneck velocity, their lives hanging on holding on to each other until they reached beyond the violent shattering that threatened every escalating moment and landed in a place where they could peacefully return to themselves again. Jake didn't care how long that took…minutes, hours.

It was a fantastic journey—her response to him, what he felt himself, a host of primal elements whipping them towards a final crescendo. The breakthrough was a totally cataclysmic moment, both of them crying out as the storm released them into a free fall of exquisite delight and they floated down on a sweet cloud of ecstasy, still clamped together as they shifted into a more relaxed embrace, prolonging what they had shared as long as they could.

Even just cuddling her close to him was sweet, smelling the scent of her hair, winding strands of it around his fingers, rubbing his cheek over its silkiness, feeling the rhythm of her breathing in the rise and fall of her breasts against his chest, the sensual stroking of one of her legs between his, knowing she was still revelling in feeling him.

Eventually thoughts drifted through Jake's mind, carrying a need to make sense of why this sexual experience with Laura had been so incredibly intense. Never before had he been completely locked into having a woman like this, driven to take, driven beyond what he'd previously known. His liaisons with other women had been more casual pleasures, enjoyable, relaxing—what he'd considered normal. Why did the animal chemistry go deeper with Laura Costarella?

She was definitely the most beautiful woman he'd ever taken to bed. Had that heightened his excitement? Somehow he couldn't quite believe that would affect him so much. His mind kept niggling at her family connection to Alex Costarella. Was it because of *who* she was, linking her to the passion for retribution, which had consumed most of his life for the past ten years? Or did the fact that she should have remained forbidden to him cause the difference?

Impossible to pin it down. All he absolutely

knew was he couldn't allow this affair to es-
calate into a serious relationship. If he kept to
that, surely he could simply enjoy what she
gave him—her companionship over the dinners he would arrange, and the intense physical pleasure they would share in bed together
afterwards.

Settling on this determination, Jake shut
down on the questions, intent on making the
most of this night together. 'Feeling good?' he
asked, wondering what she was thinking, if
she was happily satisfied with her decision to
set aside her reservations about him.

'Mmmh…very good.'

There was a smile in her voice.

He didn't need to know any more. He smiled
his own contentment with the situation.

She began an idle stroking of his body—slow,
erotic caresses, which instantly stimulated him
into touching more of her, lingering over every
voluptuous curve, loving the wonderfully sen-

sual feel of her womanliness. Touching moved into kissing as they explored each other in intimate detail, arousing the need to merge again, to feel all that could be felt between them.

It was marvellous, less frenzied this time but still incredibly exciting with the mutual abandonment of all inhibitions. It left Jake feeling flooded with pleasure, and the gradually ebbing waves of it lulled him into a deep untroubled sleep.

Laura woke to morning light. They'd forgotten to draw the curtains last night, too consumed with each other to think of anything beyond the sensational intimacy they'd shared. She rolled over to look at the man who had taken her to heights of pleasure she had never even imagined, let alone known.

He was still asleep. Despite the brilliant dark eyes being shut, his face was still strongly handsome and his body… She sighed over how perfectly manly it was, just the right amount of muscularity and everything ideally proportioned. Absolutely gorgeous. Sex appeal in spades. What a fantastic night she'd had with him! No regrets, that was for sure! Whatever happened next between them, this was one experience she would never forget.

Careful not to wake him, she slid off the bed and padded quietly to the bathroom, wanting to freshen up and look good when he did open his eyes. She grabbed her handbag off the desk in passing, glad that it contained a small hairbrush and lipstick. With no change of clothes to wear, it was a relief to find bathrobes provided for guests. She could lounge around in one of them until it was near time to leave the hotel.

Having showered and groomed herself as best she could, Laura returned to the bedroom to find Jake still asleep. Quite happy for a little time on her own, she settled on the window-seat, her back against the side wall, feet up on the cushion, arms hugging her knees, instinctively wanting to hug in all the lovely feelings generated by last night with Jake.

It wasn't just the sex, although that had been unbelievably awesome. Even now her heart swelled with the sheer joy of learning how marvellous it could be with the right man. Nothing could have felt more *right* to her, which made her wonder if it was wrong to stand back from a serious relationship with Jake. So far she liked everything he had shown of himself, and definitely wanted to know a lot more. Maybe they could have something great together.

The view of the botanical gardens caught her eye. A stroll through them would be a pleasant way of continuing the day—time to chat about their interests and look for more common ground between them. She would like to see the house he was renovating, too, the kind of home he was making for himself. The environment people chose to live in could speak volumes about them. Sharing the private life of Jake Freedman was an exciting prospect and Laura was hugging that to herself, too, when his voice broke into her hopeful reverie.

'Happy with the view this morning?'

She laughed, bubbling over with high spirits and looking at him with sparkling pleasure. 'It's lovely! The sun is shining and it's going to be a beautiful day.'

He grinned at her as he rolled out of bed, saying cheerfully, 'So let's make a start on it. Call room service and order breakfast for both of us while I freshen up in the bathroom.'

'What would you like?'

'You choose. I have great faith in your food judgement.'

He left her grinning, enjoying the back view of him as he headed off to the bathroom. Only when this vision was cut off did she swing her legs off the window-seat and set about ordering their breakfast, choosing what she wanted herself and hoping Jake would be pleased with everything.

He came out of the bathroom, wearing the other bathrobe and checking his watch. 'It's eight o'clock now. How long before room service arrives?'

'About another twenty minutes.'

The dark eyes twinkled sexily. 'Only time for a good-morning kiss then. And no disrobing.'

'We have the rest of the day,' she suggested happily as he drew her into his embrace.

He frowned. 'No. No we don't. There's work I have to get done on the house before the plumber comes tomorrow.'

'Can I help you?' she asked impulsively, wanting to be with him.

He shook his head. 'You would be a major distraction, Laura. I'll work more efficiently on my own.'

He grazed his lips over hers—a distraction that didn't quite soothe the stab of disappointment over the rejection of her offer. She told herself his reasoning was fair enough and opened her mouth for a whole-hearted kiss. He'd given her a wonderful night and there would be more in the future. No need to be greedy, asking for today, as well.

It was a soft, very sensual kiss, and he withdrew from it before it escalated into wild passion, brushing her hair tenderly from her face, smiling into her eyes. 'Thank you for last night. We'll do it again soon,' he promised her.

'Thank *you*. I'll look forward to it,' she said, inwardly craving much more from him but doing her best to accept the situation gracefully.

'I'll book a taxi to take you from the hotel to Eddie's apartment after we've had breakfast.' He stepped back from her and moved towards the telephone on the desk, asking, 'Where does he live, Laura?'

'Paddington.'

'That's handy.' He grinned at her as he picked up the receiver. 'We can share the taxi. I'll see you to his place first before going on home.'

'Where do you live?'

'Next suburb. Woollahra.'

Virtually in walking distance from Eddie's apartment, she thought, watching him make the call. She wanted to ask what street, but held her tongue, knowing she would be tempted to go there and suddenly frightened of how deeply she was being drawn by this man.

Jake didn't want a full-on relationship. He'd told her so at dinner last night. And she had been super-cautious about going down that road, too. Obviously nothing had changed for him. It shouldn't have changed for her, either. She had to keep her head straight about this, not get twisted up by emotions that could mess with the decisions she'd made about her life.

A journey with meeting places.

Best to keep to that.

But somehow she couldn't really take pleasure in the breakfast they shared. It didn't sit right in her stomach. And she hated the taxi trip to Paddington, knowing Jake was travelling on without her. It took an act of will to smile her goodbye at him. And then, of course, she had to face Eddie and say everything had been fine.

Which was the truth.

Though not quite.

It had been fantastic, brilliant, totally engaging.

Too engaging.

And that was dangerous.

CHAPTER EIGHT

To Eddie's inevitable query about her night with Jake Freedman, she breezily answered, 'Great food, great sex, and marriage is not on the menu for either of us so don't worry about my becoming a victim of secret agendas. That's definitely out!'

Later in the day, she settled her mother's concern with, 'It won't become a serious relationship, Mum. It was just a dinner date, which I might or might not repeat.' With a mischievous smile, she added, 'Depends on how good the restaurant is if he asks me out again.'

It made her mother laugh. 'Oh, you and food!'

And she cut off her father's probe into the personal connection by regaling him with details of every spicy dish she'd tasted, virtually dismissing Jake's company as pleasant enough but relatively unimportant.

However, it was easier to establish in other people's minds that an involvement with Jake was not a big issue than it was to convince herself. Life simply wasn't the same as before she met him. He dominated her thoughts, especially at night when she was alone in bed, her body restless with memories of their intense intimacy. It was impossible to block him out for long and she grew angry and frustrated with herself for not being able to set him at a sensible distance, especially as day followed day without any contact from him.

He hadn't given her *his* mobile telephone number.

He obviously had a silent land number at his Woollahra home because his name wasn't listed in the telephone directory.

No way could she call him at work because her father might get to hear about it.

Control of any connection between them was all on *his* side and she had no control whatsoever over yearning to be reconnected. Which was turning her into a stupid, love-sick cow and she hated being like that, hated it so much when he did finally call her on Friday afternoon, the zoom of pleasure at hearing his voice was speared through by resentment at his power to affect her so deeply. She only grudgingly managed a polite 'Hi!' to his greeting.

He didn't seem to notice any coldness in her response, rolling straight into the business of the call without any personal enquiries about her or her well-being. 'I've been trying all week to book us a table at one of your top restaurants for tomorrow night. Can't be done. They're all booked up and there hasn't been any cancellations. However, I have managed to get us a table at Peter Gilmore's Quay restaurant for next Saturday night. Is that okay with you?'

Peter Gilmore's Quay—listed as one of the

top fifty restaurants in the world! It was a totally irresistible invitation. A rush of excited enthusiasm flooded over all other feelings.

'Fantastic!' tripped off her tongue. 'I saw his amazing Snow Egg dessert on a television show. It started with a layer of guava purée mixed with whipped cream. On top of that was guava-flavoured crushed ice. Then a meringue shaped like an egg and an inside that was creamy custard apple. It was topped off with a thin layer of toffee melted over it. Absolutely to die for!'

His laughter flowed through her like a fountain of joy. She couldn't help smiling, couldn't help feeling happy.

'Shall we meet there at seven o'clock? Same as last time?' he asked.

'Yes.'

'Great! See you then, Laura.'

Click!

That was it from him.

The happiness deflated into a rueful sigh. It was what they had agreed upon—meetings for an adventure into fine dining. Jake probably thought of any sexual follow-up as icing on the cake. And she should, too. She couldn't fault him for not suggesting they do something else together this weekend. The problem of wanting more was entirely hers and she had to deal with it, get over it.

On the whole, Laura thought she managed that fairly well over the following week. Probably knowing they had a definite date to meet made it easier to concentrate on other things. She promised herself that at this meeting she would not expect an extension of their time together beyond the night, nor hope for it. After all, it was better for her to maintain her independence and not become slavishly besotted with the man.

Despite all her sensible reasoning, she could not control the fizz of excitement as she prepared for the big evening out. In an attempt to lessen its importance to her and show Jake she was taking this journey as casually as he was, she chose a far less dressy outfit—her best jeans, which were acceptable almost anywhere, and a peasant-style top with some wild costume jewellery she'd bought at the markets. Beaded sandals completed the look she wanted—fun, not seriously formal or serious anything else.

Eddie had been warned she would be staying overnight at his apartment again. Before leaving home she deliberately picked a yellow rose, not a red one, from her mother's garden. It was a Pal Joey rose and it had a fabulous scent. Jake might not remember asking her to bring one to their next dinner together but it definitely showed she was keeping to her side of their deal.

The ferry ride across the harbour from Mosman to Circular Quay brought her close to the site of the restaurant. There was an excited lilt in her step as she walked around to the overseas passenger terminal where all the big cruise ships docked. Jake would be waiting for her inside Quay on the upper level and tonight would undoubtedly be brilliant all over again.

For Jake it had taken rigid discipline to wait through the fortnight before indulging himself with Laura again. It would only be a week next time, and the next, and the next, provided, of course, she wanted to go on with it. Why shouldn't he have as much of her as he could within reasonable limits? As long as he kept the end in mind, his involvement with her would not get in the way of what he had to do. It was no good wishing she wasn't Alex Costarella's daughter. Nothing could change that.

She walked into the restaurant looking like a wonderfully vivid gypsy with her black curly hair all fluffed out around her shoulders, lots of colourful beads around her neck and a peasant blouse that clung to the lush fullness of her breasts. Tight jeans accentuated the rest of her sexy curves and the instant kicks to his heart and groin told Jake she was having too big an impact on him.

He shouldn't have started this.

Shouldn't be going on with it.

But she smiled at him as he stood up from their table to greet her and a rush of pleasure had him smiling back. Just before she reached him, her hand dived into the bag she carried and brought out a full-blown yellow rose.

'For you to smell,' she said, her blue eyes sparkling a flirtatious challenge.

It surprised him, delighted him, and the pleasure she brought him intensified as he took the rose and lifted it to his nose. 'Mmmh... I shall always connect this glorious scent with you.'

She laughed. 'And I shall always connect glorious food with you. I can't wait to salivate through Peter Gilmore's menu.'

He laughed and quickly held out her chair with an invitational wave. 'At your service.'

Once they were both seated, a waiter arrived, handing them menus, and Jake asked him to bring a glass of water for the rose to keep it fresh.

As soon as they were left alone together, Laura leaned forward with another heart-kicking smile. 'I'm glad you like it.'

He grinned. 'I have plans for this rose.'

'What plans?'

'For later tonight.' Like rubbing it all over her skin and breathing in the scent as he kissed her wherever he wanted. 'I've booked us a room at the Park Hyatt at Campbell Cove....'

'Another hotel,' she broke in with a frown.

'My place is still a mess,' he explained with

an apologetic grimace. 'Can't take you there, Laura.'

He never would. He *had* to keep her separate from his real life.

'But I know that hotel is terribly expensive, Jake. And on top of this dinner tonight, which will undoubtedly cost the earth...'

'The cost is not a problem to me,' he assured her.

Still she frowned. 'Does my father pay you so well?'

He shrugged. 'Well enough, but I don't count on him for my income.' *Because that was always going to end and quite soon now.* He would probably become unemployable in the bankruptcy business after he'd blown the whistle on how corrupt some of it was and he'd prepared for that outcome. 'I have a side interest that has proved very profitable.'

It piqued her curiosity. 'What is it?'

There was no harm in telling her. He doubted

she would tell her father and it didn't really matter if Costarella knew, not this close to his resignation from the company. 'I buy run-down houses, renovate them in my spare time, then sell them on.'

'Ah!' She looked pleased. 'The property ladder. That's another show I sometimes watch on TV. It's always fascinating to see how each property is improved before reselling. How many houses have you done?'

'I'm currently on my fifth.'

'I'd love to see it sometime. See what you're doing to it,' she said with eager interest.

He had to clamp down hard on the strong impulse to share it with her, to hear her views on the renovations he was doing, enjoy her interest. She was so attractive in so many ways. But anything beyond sexual intimacy had to be discouraged or he risked becoming far too hooked on Laura Costarella. Bad enough that he couldn't go to bed without wanting her in it.

'Maybe when it's further along,' he said rue-fully. 'It's virtually a shell right now. Nothing to see but mess.'

She grimaced in disappointment. 'Okay. I guess you'd prefer to feel some pride in show-ing off your work. I take it you've made a good profit from each house you've done.'

'Good enough not to worry about paying for a great night out with you, Laura, so don't you worry about it, either. I can well afford spe-cial treats like this and having you share them doubles the pleasure.'

She visibly relaxed, smiling her heart-kicking smile at him again as she picked up her menu. 'In that case, I'm very happy to share your pleasure. I shall have no inhibitions about ordering whatever I want to try.'

No inhibitions in bed, either, Jake thought happily, relieved that she wasn't pressing the house issue. Their time together had to be time out from his real life. He couldn't consider anything else with her however much he would like to.

Laura let herself wallow in the pleasure of being with Jake. He was so attractive in every respect—looks, wit, charm. There was nothing about him she didn't like. However, he was big on control, and she shouldn't forget that. Although there was a plus side to that, too. It had obviously taken a great deal of inner strength to set the trauma of losing his parents aside and drive himself towards establishing a professional career, and his enterprise in climbing the property ladder, as well, was truly admirable.

Something Eddie had said popped into her mind—*sooner or later he'll turn you off*—but she honestly couldn't see that happening, definitely not tonight. In fact, she was so turned on, it was impossible to find any wrongness in him.

He was the best company over dinner, relishing and enjoying the amazingly wonderful food as much as she did. The conversation between them was fun. The sexy twinkle in his eyes kept her excitement bubbling. She loved every bit of him, which should have set warning signals off in her head, but it was so giddy with delight, no sense of caution was even registered.

Again it was an easy walk to the hotel. Her body was humming with delicious anticipation. Her feet wanted to dance all the way. Jake had brought the rose she'd given him at the restaurant, twiddling it in his fingers as they walked, smiling down at it, and she smiled at it, too, imagining he intended taking it home with him as a romantic reminder of her.

She knew this wasn't supposed to be a romantic relationship. It was probably crazy wanting it to turn into one, yet all her female instincts were insisting this man was the right man for her. He wasn't *demanding* anything of her. It was simply great being together.

The hotel was brilliantly sited right below the harbour bridge. A set of glass doors on the far side of their room showcased a fabulous view of the opera house. Laura couldn't help loving the luxury of it, couldn't help loving the man who was giving it to her. As soon as the door was closed behind them, she turned to hug him tightly and kiss him with every fibre of her being, unable to wait another second to feel all he could make her feel.

Almost instantly they were on fire for each other, quick hungry kisses turning into fierce, needful passion. The barrier of clothes was un-bearable. She broke away to get rid of hers and laughed as she saw Jake clamping the stem of the rose between his teeth to free his hands for the same purpose.

'Just as well I picked off the thorns,' she tossed at him.

'Mmmh…' was all he could answer.

Naked and still laughing with wild exhilaration, she raced him to the bed, landing and rolling until her caught her, trapping her into stillness with one strong leg flung over hers. She looked up into wickedly glittering eyes, her chest heaving for breath, her heart hammering with excitement.

'You can't kiss me with that rose between your teeth,' she teased, her lower body wriggling provocatively against his.

He plucked the rose free and started caressing her face with it. 'I've been fantasising about doing this all evening. Lie still, Laura. Close your eyes. Feel the petals gliding over your skin. Breathe in the scent of them.'

It took enormous control to follow his instructions but it was worth the effort, focussing on the amazing sensuality of what he was doing, the soft graze of the rose, tantalisingly gentle, followed by a trail of kisses that had all her nerve ends buzzing. It made her feel like a pagan goddess being worshipped, anointed with perfume and brought to tingling life by a ceremony of slowly escalating physical ministrations.

She had never been so acutely aware of her body, hadn't realised she had erotic zones below her hip-bones, behind her knees, on the soles of her feet. To be touched like this everywhere, to be kissed as though every inch of her was adored…it was an incredible experience, mesmerising, heavenly.

Finally he came to her most intimate parts, caressing her to an exquisite tension, making it impossible for her to lie still any longer. Her body arched in need for release and she cried out his name, desperately wanting him to take her to the end now.

He moved swiftly to oblige and it was wondrous all over again, the ebb and flow of extreme sensations gathering momentum to a fantastic climax, then the delicious aftermath of sweet contentment, the scent of the yellow rose still lingering on her skin, adding its heady pleasure to their intimate togetherness.

Laura had never felt so blissfully happy. To have a lover like Jake…she was incredibly lucky to have met him. She could even find it in her heart to be grateful to her father for bringing him into her life. This journey was definitely worth taking and she hoped it would go on for a long, long time.

As they were leaving the hotel the next morning Jake asked, 'Will you be free to join me next Saturday night? I've booked a table at Universal, Christine Manfield's restaurant.'

Free for you anytime, she thought, her heart skipping with pleasure at not having to wait more than a week to be with him again. Glorious food was no longer the seductive temptation it had been, though she would absolutely enjoy it, having Jake as her dining partner.

'That would be lovely,' she said, trying not to sound too eager for his company, which was now the main drawcard. This relationship did have to be controlled. Jake was not falling all over himself to be with her every free moment he had and it was better for her if she could hold him at a distance, too, in between their meeting points,

'Same time?' he asked.

'Suits me.'

'Good!'

He gave her his brilliant, sexy smile and Laura managed a smile back though her insides clenched, wanting, needing much more of him. She had to bite down on her tongue to stop herself pleading, *Why can't we be together today? I won't get in the way of your working on the house renovations. I'll help. We can chat, laugh, enjoy being with each other.*

The words kept pounding through her mind as they settled in the taxi that would take her to

Eddie's apartment before driving on to Jake's place, but she couldn't let herself voice them. It would put Jake in a position of power over her, knowing she wanted him more than he wanted her.

Had her mother fallen into that trap with her father, showing how needy she was? If so, he'd certainly taken advantage of her vulnerability. She wasn't sure if Jake would be like that or not, but her gut feeling told her not to show any weakness that could be exploited.

It was best to keep to what they had agreed upon. If anything changed further along the line, the change had to come from him, not from her and certainly not today.

CHAPTER NINE

TETSUYA'S, a Japanese-French fusion eatery many times listed amongst the top fifty restaurants in the world, was Jake's choice for his last night with Laura. It had the longest waiting time to secure a table—two months—and he'd actually held back his own agenda, just to have this very special dinner together before he took her father down.

He checked his watch as he waited for her to arrive, conscious of not wanting her to be late, not wanting to have a minute of this final encounter wasted. It wasn't quite seven o'clock. The hell of it was he would miss the pleasure of her company, miss the fantastic sex they had shared even more, but knew it was stupid to try spinning out their time with each other any further.

It had been good. Great. But she was her father's daughter and once the axe fell on Costarella he would come out fighting for blood in return and the first casualty would be any personal association with his accuser. Laura would be turned out of the Mosman mansion if she didn't toe that line. Even if she chose not to and fled to her brother's apartment... No, she wouldn't do that. She would stay by her mother to deflect as much of her father's venom as she could.

Tonight was it—the end.

No point in looking for any way around it.

Besides, once he'd achieved the objective he'd set for himself he wanted to move on, find the kind of relationship he'd seen between his mother and stepfather, have a family of his own, hopefully sharing good times with his wife and children. Regardless of how powerfully drawn he was to Laura Costarella, he couldn't fit her into that picture.

As hot she was in bed, she kept a cool head out of it, content to go about her own life without trying to get him involved in it. This was confirmation to Jake that marriage had no appeal to her—understandable given *her* family background. Part-time lovers was as far as any man would get with Laura. It made the end of their affair easier in so far as he knew it carried no deep importance to her. He'd given her pleasure. He hoped the memory of it would not get too tainted by the angst his actions would inevitably cause in the Costarella household.

All this past week he'd been tossing up whether to tell her, warn her what was about to happen, explain why. Somehow that smacked too much of justifying himself and he didn't need to do that, not when he was meting out justice, which would eventually be evident to everyone. Besides, he'd told Laura right from the beginning he didn't want to want to her. Understanding would come soon enough. Better for them both to enjoy this one last night.

Laura was smiling, aglow with excited anticipation as she entered Tetsuya's. She was ten minutes late, due to the public transport connections needed to get to Kent Street in the inner city—where the restaurant was located—but she was finally here for another night with Jake. And there he was, rising from the table where he'd been seated.

Her heart skipped a beat. Every time he had this impact. And his smile of pleasure on seeing her…it was like a fountain of joy bursting through her. She loved this man, loved being with him, fiercely wished they could be sharing much more than one night a week.

Though she told herself it was sensible not to get too involved, not when she still had to earn her university degree. It was halfway through the year now. In a few more months… Was Jake waiting for her to be fully qualified before inviting her into more of his life? There was quite an age gap between them. Maybe he was conscious of that, too. Whatever his reasons for keeping their relationship so strictly limited, Laura felt sure they would wear out eventually. They were too good together—great together—for this journey to ever end.

She couldn't resist planting a greeting kiss on his cheek before sitting down. 'Sorry I'm a bit late. The bus trip was slow. Lots of people getting on and off.'

'No problem,' he assured her, his deep rich voice curling around her heart, warming it with pleasure. 'You're here. And I've been perusing the menu. This promises to be a fantastic dining experience.'

'Oh, wow! I've been *so* looking forward to it.'

He laughed at her excitement as they both

took their seats. Laura loved his laugh, the sexy male rumble of it, the way it lit up his handsome face, the dancing twinkles in his eyes.

'I want us to do the gustatory menu—all eight courses of it. Are you up for it?' he asked.

Laura goggled at him. 'Eight courses!'

'They won't be big. Just a marvelous range of tastes.'

'Let me see.' She held out her hand for the menu and he passed it over. The list of dishes Jake wanted proved irresistible. 'I'm up for it,' she said decisively.

It would obviously cost Jake another small fortune, but also obviously he didn't care so Laura refused to feel guilty about the expense. It was his choice. He grinned at her, knowing she was happy to succumb to temptation.

She sighed. 'You're spoiling me rotten with all this, Jake.'

An oddly rueful expression twisted his grin. 'You've given me more than money can buy, Laura. I should probably thank you for being you.'

Why did that sound…almost as if he was saying goodbye to her? Laura frowned over the uncomfortable niggle. Surely he was just trying to balance out what they had together, make it feel okay to her. 'It's no big deal being me,' she said critically.

He shook his head, his eyes gently mocking her. 'I can't imagine enjoying our dinners so much with anyone else.'

She relaxed into a relieved smile. 'Then I should thank you for being you because I can't imagine it, either.'

'Good to be in accord on that point.'

She laughed. 'I think we're in accord on many points.'

'True. Shall we order now?'

He signalled their readiness to a waiter while Laura happily assured herself that everything was fine between them.

Again it was another brilliant evening with Jake. The dinner was sensational. It was great fun enjoying and discussing the various tastes, comparing it to what they'd eaten in other restaurants. Laura visited the ladies' room just before they were about to leave and on her way back to their table, she was struck by another little stab of uncertainty.

Jake was not looking for her return. He sat in pensive mode, a dark, bleak expression wiping out all the sparkles he'd shot her way during dinner. It didn't take much intuition to realise something was wrong—something in the private life he didn't share with her. Wasn't it time that he did? They'd been seeing each other on a very intimate basis for almost three months now. Surely he knew her well enough to trust her with what was in his mind.

He brightened as she reached the table, pulling himself back from the place he'd travelled to without her, but Laura's fighting spirit had been pricked into taking a stand. 'What were you thinking of just now, Jake?'

He shook his head, a wry little smile curling his mouth as he rose from his chair. 'A piece of the past. Nothing to do with you, Laura. I've called a taxi for us. It's waiting outside.'

He tucked her arm around his as she frowned over his evasive reply. 'I want to know,' she said, shooting him a searching look.

He grimaced at her obstinacy, but did answer her. 'I was thinking of my parents. How much they enjoyed sharing meals together.'

'Oh!' Laura's heart instantly lifted. The memory had obviously saddened Jake but she felt it did have something to do with her—a connection to what *they* were doing, which he enjoyed with her! It made her feel their relationship was more meaningful to him than he was willing to admit at this point.

'I've booked us into the Park Hotel tonight,'

he told her as they made their exit from the restaurant.

Another hotel. She knew it overlooked Hyde Park in the city centre, which gave them only a short trip to Paddington and Woollahra in the morning. It always disappointed her that he didn't ask her home with him but she'd decided never to push it. Besides, she was still cherishing that link to his parents, whom he'd loved very much.

They didn't chat in the taxi. Laura was keenly anticipating the sexual connection with Jake and she imagined his mind was occupied with it, too. It seemed to her he held her hand more tightly than usual, his long fingers strongly interlaced with hers, their pads rubbing her palm. She silently craved more skin-to-skin contact, barely controlling her impatience to dive into bed with him.

Certainly their desire for each other hadn't waned at all. As soon as the door of the hotel room was closed behind them they were locked in a fierce embrace, kissing like there was no tomorrow, shedding clothes as fast as they could on their way to the bed, totally consumed with a wild passion that demanded to be slaked before easing into a more sensual love-making.

Even that seemed to carry more intensity than usual, more need for continually intimate contact, and Laura revelled in it, believing it meant Jake felt more for her now, on a personal rather than just a sexual level. It was a long time before they fell asleep and in the morning she woke to the sense of having her body being softly caressed by a loving hand. She rolled over to fling her arm around Jake, who proceeded to arouse her more acutely. They'd never had sex *the morning after* but they did this time, and Laura took it as another heart-hugging sign that their relationship was beginning to change to a closer one.

They ate a very hearty breakfast.

Showered, dressed and ready to leave, they were at the door of their hotel room when Jake turned and kissed her again, a long, passionate kiss that left Laura tingling with excitement on their elevator ride down to the foyer. Her mind swam with the hope he was going to ask her home with him instead of their going separate ways today.

A taxi was waiting outside the hotel entrance. Jake opened the passenger door for her and she got in, sliding along the back seat to make room for him. Instead of following her he leaned in to tell the driver Eddie's address and hand him a twenty dollar note.

Startled, Laura blurted, 'Aren't you coming with me?'

His dark eyes met hers, flat dark, almost black, devoid of any brilliance. 'No. I have somewhere else to go, Laura,' he stated decisively. He reached out and touched her cheek. 'It's been good. Thank you.'

Then the brief caress was withdrawn, as swiftly as Jake withdrew himself, shutting the passenger door and signalling the driver to take her away. Which he did, given no reason not to.

Laura was too stunned to protest the move. She sat in total shock, her hopes, her dreams, her expectations crashing around her. That was a goodbye! Not a *see you next time.* Jake hadn't mentioned a next time. Her hand lifted and clapped her cheek, holding on to what a creeping tide of panic was telling her had been his farewell touch.

Her mind railed over why it should be so. Surely there was no reason to give up what had been good. He would call her during the week. This couldn't be the end. Yet the more she thought about it, the more she felt he had been saying goodbye to her all last night. And this morning. Last dinner, last sex, last kiss, last touch!

But maybe she had it wrong. Maybe, maybe…

The taxi pulled up outside Eddie's apartment. Laura pulled herself out of her mental torment enough to thank the driver and step out onto the pavement. A glance at her watch showed almost eleven o'clock. She hoped Eddie was having a Sunday brunch with his friends somewhere because she wasn't up to chatting normally with him, not when her mind kept running on this awful emotional treadmill.

No such luck!

He was seated at his dining table in the living room, a cup of coffee to hand as he perused the newspapers. The moment she let herself into the apartment he looked up to shoot an opening line at her. 'Hi! Had another great night with Dad's golden boy?'

'Yes. A great night.' Even to her own ears it was a hollow echo of Eddie's words. It was impossible to work any happy enthusiasm into her voice.

He looked at her quizzically. 'Tetsuya's up to your expectations?'

'Yes. Absolutely.' That was better, more emphatic.

'Are you sick or something?'

'No.'

He sat back in his chair and gave her his wise look. 'Then why do you look like death warmed up, Laura?'

She sighed, accepting the fact there was very little she could hide from Eddie. He had a very shrewd talent for boring straight through any camouflage she put up. 'I think Jake said goodbye to me this morning and I'm not ready to say goodbye to him,' she said, shrugging in an attempt to minimise her dilemma.

Eddie grimaced and rose from his chair, waving her to the table. 'Come and sit down. I'll get you a cup of coffee. It might perk you up a bit.'

She slumped into a chair, feeling weirdly drained of energy.

'Why do you *think* he said goodbye?' Eddie asked as he poured coffee from the percolator.

Laura relived the scene in her mind. 'He put me into the taxi at the hotel, touched my cheek and said, "It's been good. Thank you." Usually he shares the taxi with me and tells me where we'll meet next week, but this morning he shut the door on me and waved me off.'

'It's *been* good,' Eddie repeated, musing over the past tense. He shook his head as he brought her the shot of caffeine and resumed his seat across the table from her. 'If he'd said *was* good...'

'No, it was *been* good. I'm not mistaken about that, Eddie.'

He grimaced. 'Got to say it sounds like a cut-off line to me. Do you have any idea why?'

'No. None. Which is why I'm so...in a mess about it.'

'No little niggles about how he was responding to you? Like maybe getting bored with the routine you'd established?'

'I'm not stupid, Eddie. I'd know if he was bored,' she cried, though right now she didn't feel certain about anything.

'Okay. He wasn't bored but he was saying goodbye regardless of the pleasures you both shared. That only leaves one motive, Laura,' Eddie said ruefully.

'What?'

'You've served your purpose.'

She shook her head in helpless confusion. 'I don't understand. What purpose?'

'You can bet it's something to do with dear old Dad.'

'But we've kept our whole relationship away from him,' she protested.

'You have, but how can you possibly know that Jake has?'

'He promised me...'

'Laura, Laura…' Eddie looked pained. 'I warned you from the start that this is a guy who plays all the angles. He's not our father's right-hand man for nothing. He's obviously worked at winning Dad's trust. He's worked at winning yours. But let me remind you, James Bond plays his own game and I think you've just been treated to one of them—*love 'em and leave 'em.*'

James Bond… She'd stopped connecting Jake to the legendary 007 character. He was the man she wanted, the man she loved, the man she'd dreamed of having for the rest of her life. Had she been an absolute fool, getting so caught up with him? Hadn't Jake felt anything for her beyond the desire to take her to bed? How could the strong feelings he'd stirred in her be completely one-sided?

The intensity of his love-making last night and this morning had made her believe he felt a lot for her. Eddie had to be wrong. She couldn't think of any purpose Jake could have in loving her and leaving her. He might very well have somewhere else he had to be this morning— somewhere he wished he didn't have to go because of wanting to be with her—and that past tense he'd used could have been simply a slip of the tongue. Maybe she'd worked herself into a stew for nothing and he would call her during the week.

Eddie shook his head at her. 'You don't want to believe it, do you?'

'I guess time will tell, Eddie,' she said flatly. 'Let's leave it at that. Okay?'

'Okay.' He gave her a sympathetic look. 'In the meantime, chalk up the positives. You've had the experience of dining in some of the finest restaurants, staying in very classy hotels, plus a fair chunk of great sex. Not a bad three months, Laura.'

She managed a wry smile. 'No, not bad at all.'

But I want more.
Much more of Jake Freedman.
And I desperately hope I get more.

CHAPTER TEN

THE rest of Sunday went by without a call from Jake.

No contact from him on Monday, either.

It would probably come on Friday, Laura told herself, doing her best to concentrate on her uni lectures and not get too disturbed by the lack of the communication she needed. Regardless of the situation with Jake, she still had to move on with her life, get the qualifications necessary for her chosen career. Yet all her sensible reasoning couldn't stop the sick yearning that gripped her stomach when her thoughts drifted to him. And telling herself he would call soon didn't help.

It surprised her to see her father's car parked in the driveway when she arrived home on

Tuesday afternoon. He never left work early and it wasn't even five o'clock. A scary thought hit her. Had something bad happened to her mother? An accident? Illness? She couldn't imagine anything but an emergency bringing her father home at this hour.

She ran to the front door, her heart pumping with fear as she unlocked it and rushed into the hallway. 'Mum? Dad?' she called anxiously.

'Get in here, Laura!' her father's voice thundered from the lounge room. 'I've been waiting for you!'

She stood stock-still, her heart thumping even harder. He was in a rage. No distress in that tone. It was total fury. The only concern she need have for her mother was being subjected to his venom again.

The double doors from the hallway into the lounge room were open. Laura stiffened her spine, squared her shoulders and forced her feet forward, knowing that her mother would be spared the full-on brunt of savage remarks when he turned them onto her. It didn't matter how much she hated these vicious scenes. Better for her to be here than not here.

On entering the war zone, she found her mother cowering in the corner of one of the sofas, white-faced and hugging herself tightly as though desperately trying to hold herself together. Her father was standing behind the bar, splashing Scotch into a glass of ice. *His* face was red and the bottle of Scotch was half-empty.

'Are you still seeing Jake Freedman?' he shot at her.

No point in trying any evasion when her father was in this mood. He'd dig and dig and dig.

'I don't know,' she answered honestly.

'What do you mean "you don't know"?' he jeered, his eyes raking her with contempt. 'Don't pretend to be stupid, Laura.'

She shrugged. 'I was with him on Saturday night but he made no plans for us to meet again.'

Her father snorted. 'Had a last hurrah, screwing my daughter.'

'Alex, it's not Laura's fault,' her mother spoke up, showing more courage than she usually did. 'You introduced him to her.'

It enraged him into yelling, 'The bloody mole played his cards perfectly! Anyone would have been sucked in by him!'

'Then don't blame Laura,' her mother pleaded weakly, wilting under the blast.

What had Jake done? Laura's mind was in a whirl as she crossed the room to where her mother was scrunched into as small a space as possible and sat on the sofa's wide armrest next to her. 'What's going on, Dad?' she asked, needing to get to the crux of the problem.

He bared his teeth in a vicious snarl. 'That bastard has taken all my business to the Companies' Auditors and Liquidators Disciplinary Board and had me suspended from any further practice in the industry, pending further investigation.'

'Suspended?' This was why he was home, but… 'Investigation of what?'

His hand sliced the air in savage dismissal. 'You've never been interested in my work, Laura, so it's none of your concern.'

'I want to know what Jake is accusing you of.'

He shook a furious finger at her. 'All you have to know is he was hell-bent on taking me down every minute he was supposedly working *for* me. Rolling you was icing on the cake for him.'

'But why? You're making it sound like a personal vendetta.'

'It *is* a personal vendetta.' His eyes bitterly raked her up and down. 'How personal can you get with his hands all over you, exulting in taking every damned liberty he could.'

'Alex!' her mother cried in pained protest.

She was ignored.

'And you let him, didn't you? My daughter!' her father thundered.

Laura refused to answer.

He sneered at her silence. 'He would have revelled in every intimacy you gave up to him.'

'This isn't about me, Dad,' she said as calmly as she could. 'I'm obviously a side issue. Why does Jake have a personal vendetta against you?'

'Because of JQE!' The words were spat out.

'That doesn't mean anything to me,' Laura persisted.

He glared at her contemptuously as though her ignorance was another poisonous barb to his pride.

Her chin lifted defiantly. 'I think I have the right to know what I've been a victim of.'

'JQE was his stepfather's company,' he finally informed her in a bitterly mocking tone. 'He believes I could have saved it and chose not to. The man died of a heart attack soon after I secured the liquidator's fee.'

*Step*father! 'Was his surname different to Jake's?'

'Of course it was! If I'd had any idea they were related, he would never have been employed by me.'

'How long has he been working in your company?'

'Six years! Six damnable years of worming his way through my files, wanting to nail me to the wall!'

A man with a mission…James Bond… Dark and dangerous…

Her instincts had been right at their first meeting, but she hadn't heeded them, hadn't wanted to.

'Could you have saved his stepfather's company, Dad?' she asked, wanting to know if the mission was for justice or some twisted form of vengeance. Jake had loved his stepfather, possibly the only father he had known.

'The man was an idiot, getting in over his head,' her father snarled. 'Even with help he was in no state to rescue anything. His wife was dying of cancer. Trying to hang on was stupid.'

A judgement call. Had it been right or a deliberate choice for her father to make a profit out of it, charging huge fees to carry out the liquidation process?

What was the truth?

Laura knew she wouldn't get it from her father. He would serve his own ends. Always had.

As for Jake, he must have been totally torn up with grief when the seeds of his mission had been sown—his mother dying of cancer, his stepfather driven into bankruptcy and dying of a heart attack. It must have been a terribly traumatic time, having to bury both parents in the midst of everything being sold up around him. She had sensed the darkness in him, seen signs of it, heard it in his voice that first day in the garden when he'd described the terrible downside of bankruptcy, but hadn't known how deep it went, hadn't known that she was connected to it by being her father's daughter.

The bottle of Scotch took another hit. A furious finger stabbed at her again. 'Don't you dare take his side in this bloody whistle-blowing or you are out of this house, Laura! He used you. Used you to show me up as even more of a fool for trusting him with my daughter.'

Had that been Jake's intention behind tempting her into an affair? An iron fist squeezed her heart. He'd controlled every aspect of their meetings, kept their involvement limited to Saturday nights. Had he been secretly revelling in having her whenever he called? Because of who she was?

'What there was between us is over,' she said flatly.

'It had better be, my girl!' Threat seethed through every word. 'If he contacts you…'

'He won't.' Laura was certain of it. He *had* been saying goodbye on Sunday morning.

'Don't bet on it! It would be an extra feather in his cap if he sucked you in again.'

'He won't,' she repeated, sick to her soul. She'd loved him, truly deeply loved him, and the thought of having been used to drive a dagger further into her father was devastating.

'You be damned sure of it, Laura, because if I ever find out otherwise, you'll pay for it!'

'I'm sure.'

'You're looking sick around the gills. He got to you all right.'

The savage mutter was followed by another hefty swig of Scotch.

'I'm not feeling well,' her mother said shakily. 'Will you help me up to my bedroom, Laura?'

''Course I will.' She quickly moved off the armrest to give support.

'Running away as usual,' her father said scathingly. 'We'll be living with this hanging over our heads for months, Alicia. No escaping it.'

'It's just the shock, Dad,' Laura threw back at him. 'Mum needs some recovery time.'

'Recovery! I'll never recover from this! Never! That bastard has me hamstrung!'

Not for nothing, Laura thought as she helped her mother from the room. Jake must have presented a considerable body of hard evidence against her father for him to be suspended from practice. And had still been gathering it while he was seeing her on the side.

She needed recovery time, too.

Her mother felt terribly frail. Laura put her

to bed and tucked the doona around her. 'It's not your fault, either, Mum,' she said gently.

The pale blue eyes were teary and fearful. She grasped Laura's hand. 'I don't think I can bear it if your father is home every day.'

'You don't have to. Eddie would take you in. You have only to ask.'

She shook her head fretfully. 'It wouldn't be fair on him. You don't understand, Laura. Your father wouldn't tolerate my leaving him. He'd…do something.'

Laura hated the fear but she knew there was no reasoning against it. She and Eddie had tried many times. 'Well, I don't think Dad will be at home all the time. He'll be out networking with people, fighting this situation with everything in his power.'

'Yes. Yes, he will. Thank you, Laura. I'm sorry…sorry that Jake…'

'Let's not talk about him. You just rest, Mum.'

She kissed the slightly damp forehead and left the room before her own tears welled up and spilled over—tears of hurt and shock and grief that pride had insisted she hold back in front of her father. And her mother.

In the safe haven of her bedroom she wept until she was totally drained of tears. Her mind was wiped blank for a long time as she lay in limp misery, but gradually it began to turn over everything that had happened between her and Jake in the light of what she now knew and it kept coming back to the one line that felt critically important—the line he'd spoken after their first kiss in the garden.

I don't want to want you.

But he had.

He most definitely had wanted her, and quite possibly not because of who she was but *in spite of* who she was.

Which made a huge difference to her father's

interpretation of Jake's conduct where she was concerned.

It meant she was not part of his vengeance plot.

She was an innocent connection to the man whom he saw as the prime cause of the darkest time of his life. The words he'd used describing bankruptcy came back to her—lives crumbling, futures shattered, depression so dark there is no light. The emotional intensity that had surprised her in that forceful little speech had obviously erupted from personal experience.

Looking back, she began to make much more sense of how Jake had run their affair, always keeping the end in sight, ensuring their involvement was limited, not escalating into something too serious. He'd known it was ill-fated from the start, but he'd found her as irresistible as she'd found him and he'd taken the small window of opportunity for them to enjoy each other before circumstances made it impossible.

It's been good. Thank you.

He hadn't been *using* her.

They'd both chosen to give themselves the pleasure of mutual desire and it had been good. The more Laura reasoned it out, the more she believed the journey they'd taken together was completely separate from the road Jake had been travelling to put her father out of business.

She remembered the intensity of his love-making on Saturday night, the long passionate kiss before they left the hotel room, the flat darkness—no...light—of his eyes as he touched her cheek in the taxi.

Maybe he hadn't wanted to say goodbye.

Maybe he loved her as deeply as she loved him.

Maybe he just couldn't see a future for them, given what he was about to do.

That might be true…or it might not.

It depended on how much he felt for her.

She had to see him, talk to him, find out the truth.

CHAPTER ELEVEN

LAURA wished she could have borrowed Eddie's car to tour the streets of Woollahra, looking for the houses that were being renovated, noting them down for further investigation. It would have been the most time efficient way of searching for Jake's current home, but she knew her brother would not have been sympathetic to her quest. Better not to ask. Better to go on foot, however long it took.

When she'd broken the news to Eddie, he'd leapt to the same interpretation of Jake's interest in her as her father, being quite smug about having been right that Laura should never have *gone there*, right about Jake having a mission, too. The latter was impossible to deny, but

Laura could not set aside the need to *go there* again.

At least Eddie had taken their mother out today, giving her a break from the wretched tensions at home. It left Laura enough free time to cover a fair bit of ground in her search, though it was now Sunday—no tradesmen's trucks around to mark possibilities. After three hours of walking one street after another, and feeling somewhat dispirited at her lack of success, she decided to take a break for lunch and give her feet a rest.

Heading up another street that led to a public park where she could sit and eat her home-made sandwiches, Laura could hardly believe her eyes when she actually spotted Jake. He was on the upstairs balcony of a terrace house, painting the iron-lace railings—the same shade of green as the front door and the window frames. It was a rich forest green that looked really good against the old red bricks of the house.

He looked good, too, a fact her heart was registering by thumping painfully. She stood still, staring up at him, wracked by a terrible uncertainty now that the moment of truth was at hand. Was she being an utter fool, coming to him like this? So what if she was, she fiercely argued to herself. A sharp dose of humiliation wouldn't kill her. And she wasn't about to die wondering, either.

His head lifted, his gaze suddenly swinging to her as though some invisible force had drawn it. 'Laura!' He spoke her name in a tone of angst, jerking up from his crouched position on the balcony, frowning down at her. 'What are you doing here?'

'I need to talk to you,' she blurted out.

He shook his head. 'It won't do you any good.' His gaze shot to a van parked on the other side of the street. 'That's been here since

Wednesday. I'd say your father has me under surveillance and he won't like getting a report of your coming to me. Just keep walking and maybe nothing will come of it.'

Her father's threat jangled through her mind—*you'll pay for it.*

Right now Laura didn't care. Jake had just proved his caring for her. That was more important than anything else. Or was he just trying to get her out of his life again as fast as possible?

'I have to know,' she said with immovable determination. 'I won't go until you lay out the truth to me.'

A pained grimace twisted his mouth as his hand waved in a sharp, dismissive gesture. 'You already know it had to come to an end. Remember it for what it was and move on.'

'What was it, Jake?'

'You know that, too,' he shot back at her.

'No, I don't. You kept me in the dark about

what meant most to you. I don't know if it gave you a thrill to have me while plotting to bring my father down, if I was some kind of sweet icing on the cake for you. I want to know that before I move on.'

Jake stared at the woman he should never have touched, his mind torn by the deep hurt emanating from her. She was still the most beautiful, most desirable woman he'd ever known, quite possibly would ever know, and he hated having to part from her. It had to be done, but did it have to be done with her mind poisoned against what they'd shared?

He wanted her to have a good memory of him, not a bitter one. Yet how was he to soothe the hurt and protect her from her father's wrath at the same time? The surveillance man was surely watching, taking note of this encounter. The longer it went on, the worse it would be for Laura at home.

'There's a public park at the end of this street,' he said, pointing the direction as though she had asked for it.

'I know!' she cried in exasperation. 'Can't you just answer me?'

He shot a warning look at the van. 'I'll meet you there when I've finished this painting. Go, Laura. Go now.'

He turned his attention to the work in hand, bending down to the tin of paint again, hoping the intense urgency in his voice would spur her into moving away from him. After a few moments' hesitation that tied his gut into knots, she did walk on, hopefully proving there was nothing in this meeting worth reporting.

He maintained a steady pace with the brushwork, exhibiting no haste to finish the job. It gave him time to think, time to reason out he should keep his answers to Laura short, avoid the tempting impulse to take her in his arms and prove his passion for her had been real, was still real. The ache in his groin had to be ignored. This meeting had to be limited to setting her straight, then letting her go. Anything else could not be sustained in the climate of her father's venomous animosity.

The narrow alley that ran along the back of this row of terraces allowed him to leave his house unobserved. He would return the same way. A last meeting. No more.

He does care for me. He does.

It was like a chant of joy in Laura's mind, making every step towards the park a light one for her tired feet. Jake would have no reason at all to give himself the trouble of meeting with her if she meant nothing to him. If she'd been part of his vendetta against her father, he would have shamed her in the street. He had certainly not been amused by her coming to him nor titillated by his power to draw her. He'd been pained by her presence, reminding him of what they'd shared, what he'd been trying to shut out as finished.

Except it wasn't.

Not for her and not for him.

The connection was too strong to obliterate.

Laura was sure of it.

She found a park bench under a tree and sat down to wait, not bothering to unpack the sandwiches in her handbag. Her heart was too full of other needs for eating to be a priority anymore. Jake would come to her soon—Jake, whom she loved…whom she would always love. Did he feel the same way about her? Was it only the situation with her father that had driven him to break it off with her?

She had no idea how long she waited. Her mind was obsessed with finding some way to continue their relationship—safe places to meet, secret places, whatever it took for their journey not to end. When she spotted him approaching her at a fast stride she leapt to her feet, barely quelling the urge to run to him and fling her arms around his neck. Talking had to come first, she told herself, though if he wrapped her in his embrace…

He didn't. There was no smile on his face, no joy at seeing her, no sexy twinkle in his eyes. When he reached her he took hold of her hands, squeezing them as though to prevent any other touching. 'I never meant you to be hurt, Laura,' he said gruffly. 'I thought we could simply satisfy ourselves with the pleasures we could give each other. None of that had anything to do with your father. It was all about you, the woman I wanted to be with, not whose daughter you are.'

His thumbs were dragging across the skin on the back of her hands, wanting his words to sink in, go deep, expel the nastiness of the motivation that her father had given him. The earnest sincerity in his voice, the blaze of need to convince her in his eyes... Laura believed he spoke the truth. She *wanted* to believe.

'You should have told me what you were about to do, Jake,' she blurted out. 'It wouldn't have been so bad if you'd told me.'

His mouth twisted into a rueful grimace. 'I didn't want to spoil our last night together, bringing your father into it, bringing my family background into it. And telling you wasn't going to change anything.'

'It would have prepared me.'

'Yes. I see that now. I'm sorry. I thought you'd understand. What we had was time out of time, Laura.' He squeezed her hands hard. 'You must let it go and move on.'

'I don't want to, Jake. It was too good to let go. You must feel that, too,' she pleaded.

He jerked his head in a sharp negative. 'There's no way. Your father will see to that and bucking him would make things much worse for both you and your mother. You told me she needs you. And you still have to get your uni degree for the career you want. Any association with me will cost you too much.'

If he was under surveillance… Yes, it would be too risky. The tensions at home were volatile enough already. Yet letting this connection she felt with Jake go… Everything inside her railed against giving it up.

'What about when this is all over, Jake. Could we pick up again then?'

He shook his head but there was a pained expression on his face as he answered, 'The process of indicting your father for corruption may go on for years, Laura.'

'Is he guilty?'

'Without a doubt.'

'Will he go to jail?'

'He'll be ousted from the industry. It's unlikely that any further action will be taken.'

No relief for her mother. No escape unless…

'Once I get my degree and hopefully a well-paid position, I'll be independent. And perhaps I can persuade my mother to come and live with me. We'll be free and clear of my father.'

'Perhaps...' he repeated, but there was no belief in his eyes.

Her hope for at least some distant future with him was being crushed. It begged for a chance to survive. 'Do you really want this to be good-bye, Jake?'

'No. But I can't honestly see any good way forward,' he said flatly.

'You have my mobile phone number. You could call me from time to time, check on how things are going,' she suggested, trying to keep a note of desperation out of her voice.

He wrenched his gaze from the plea in hers and stared down at their linked hands. Again his thumbs worked over her skin. After a long nerve-tearing silence, he muttered, 'You should close the door on me, Laura. You'll meet someone else with no history to make your life difficult.'

'I won't meet anyone else like you,' she said fiercely, every instinct fighting for a love she might never feel with any other man.

He expelled a long breath with the whisper, 'Nor I, you.' Then he visibly gathered himself, head lifting, meeting her gaze squarely again. 'I won't call you from time to time. I won't keep any hold on you. When I'm done with your father—however long that takes— I'll catch up with you to see where you are in your life and how we feel about each other then.'

She knew there was no fighting the hard decision in his eyes, in his voice. 'Promise me you'll do that, Jake. Whatever happens between now and then, promise me we'll meet again.'

'I promise.' He leaned forward to press a soft warm kiss on her forehead. 'Stay strong, Laura,' he murmured.

Before she could say or do anything, he'd backed off, released her hands and was walking away. She stared at his retreating figure, feeling the distance growing between them with each step he took, hating it yet resigned to the inevitability of this parting.

He'd promised her they'd meet again.

It might be years away but she didn't believe any length of time would make a difference to how she felt with him.

And she did have things to achieve—her qualifications, building a career and hopefully persuading her mother that there was another life to be led, free of abuse and oppression.

It would not be time wasted.

She would be better equipped to continue a journey with Jake Freedman when they met again—older, stronger, more his equal in everything. She could wait for that.

CHAPTER TWELVE

STAY STRONG...

Laura repeated those words to herself many times as she tried to minimise her father's savagery over the next few weeks, protecting her mother from it as best she could. She had half expected a vicious blow-up about her visit to Jake's house, but that didn't eventuate. Either there hadn't been a surveillance man at all, or he hadn't reported the incident, not seeing anything significant in it.

Strangely enough her mind was more at peace with Jake's promise. She didn't fret over his absence from her life. It was easier to concentrate on her landscape projects than when she was seeing him each week. Knowing what he was doing, knowing why, helped a lot, as did good memories when she went to bed at night. Besides, there was hope for a future with him, which she kept to herself, not confiding it to her mother or Eddie, both of whom would probably see it as an unhealthy obsession with the man.

She spent as much time with her mother as her uni studies and part-time receptionist work would allow. Nick Jeffries seemed to be finding a lot of maintenance jobs that had to be done, coming to the house two or three times a week. Laura wondered if he knowingly provided a buffer between her parents, giving her mother an excuse to be outside with him, supervising the work. He was a cheerful man, good to have around, in sharp contrast to her father, who was never anything but nasty now.

One evening she was in the kitchen with her mother, helping to prepare dinner, when he arrived home bellowing, 'Laura!' from the hallway, the tone alone warning he was bent on taking a piece out of her.

Her heart jumped. What had she done wrong? Nothing she could think of. 'I'm in the kitchen, Dad!' she called out, refusing to go running to him or show any fear of his mean temper.

Stay strong...

She kept cutting up the carrots, only looking up when he announced his entry by snidely commenting, 'Good sharp knife! You might want to stick it into someone, Laura.'

Like him? He had a smug smile on his face, in no doubt whatsoever that she wouldn't attack him physically. He was the one who had the power to hurt and that knowledge glittered in his eyes. He stood there, gloating over whatever he had in mind to do. Laura waited, saying nothing, aware that her mother had also stopped working and was tensely waiting for whatever was coming next.

'I've had Jake Freedman under surveillance,' he announced.

The visit to Jake's house! But that was so long ago. It didn't make sense that her father would keep such a tasty titbit until now.

He waved a large envelope at her. 'Hard evidence of what a slime he is.' He strolled forward, opening the envelope and removing what looked like large photographs, and laid them down on the island bench in front of her.

'Thought you'd like to see Jake Freedman's steady screw, Laura,' he said mockingly, pointing to a curvy blonde in a skimpy, skin-tight aerobic outfit, her arms locked around Jake's neck, her body pressed up against his, as was her face for a kiss.

It was like a kick in the gut, seeing him with another woman.

'Meets her at the gym three times a week.'

Every word was like a drop of acid eating into her heart.

The pointing finger moved to the next photograph. 'Goes back to her place for extra exercise.'

There was the blonde again, the pony-tail for the gym released so that her shiny hair fell around her face and shoulders in soft waves. It was a very pretty face. She was opening the door of a house, smiling back invitingly at Jake, who was paused at the foot of the steps leading up to the front porch.

'Woman works at a club on Saturday nights,' her father went on. 'Very handy. Left him free to have his delectable little encounters with you. Shows what a two-faced bastard he is in every respect.'

She didn't speak, couldn't speak. Sickening waves of shock were rolling through her. It was a huge relief that her father didn't wait for some comment from her.

'Need a drink to drown the scumbag out,' he muttered and headed off to make his usual inroads into a bottle of whisky, leaving the damning photographs behind to blast any faith she might have in Jake's love for her.

Laura stared at them. It was only a month since her meeting in the park with him—a meeting he hadn't wanted, a meeting to ensure she wouldn't pester him again, coming to his house where she had never been invited. She had accepted his reasoning, believed in his promise, and here he was with another woman, enjoying her company, having sex with her.

Two-faced…

Of course he had to be good at that—brilliant—to fool her father.

Fooling her, too, had probably been a fun exercise in comparison.

A dark, dangerous man… She should have trusted that instinct, should have said no to him, should never have allowed him to play his game with her because it had been *his* game all along, *his* arrangements, *his* rules. She had read into them what she wanted to believe and he had let her with his rotten promise.

Tears welled up and blurred her vision. She shut her eyes, didn't see her mother move to wrap her in a comforting hug, only felt the arms turning her around, a hand curling around her head and pressing it onto a shoulder. She wasn't strong in that moment, couldn't find any strength at all. She gave in to a storm of weeping until it was spent, then weakly stayed in her mother's embrace, soaking up the real love coming to her from the rubbing of her back and the stroking of her hair.

'I'm sorry you've been so hurt by this,' her mother murmured. 'Sorry you were caught up in your father's business, in past deeds you had nothing to do with. So wrong…'

'I loved him, Mum. I thought he loved me. He promised me we'd meet again when this was all over,' she spilled out, needing to unburden the pain of the soul-sickening deception.

'Perhaps that was a kinder way of letting you down than telling you the truth. You're a wonderful person, Laura. Even he had to see that, care for you a little.'

'Oh, Mum! It's such a mess!' She lifted her head and managed a wobbly smile. 'I'm a mess. Thanks for being here for me.'

Her mother returned an ironic little smile as she lifted her hand to smear the wetness from Laura's cheeks. 'As you are for me. But please don't think you always have to be, my dear. I want you to have a life of your own, away from here. Like Eddie.'

'Well, we'll talk about that when I'm through uni. Now let's do this dinner. I don't want Dad to know I've been upset.'

Pride lent her strength again. She snatched up the photographs. 'I'll just take these up to my room as reminders of my stupidity, clean myself up and be right back down to help. And don't worry about me, Mum. I'll be okay now.'

She dumped the photographs on her bed, bitterly thinking how *easy* she had been for Jake, how vulnerable she had been to his strong sex appeal, how willing to go along with *his* journey, letting him call all the shots. He'd probably had this other woman all along. Even if the pretty blonde was only a more recent acquisition for his sex life, the very fact of her spelled out that he felt no deep attachment to Alex Costarella's daughter.

Washing her face, she wished she could wash Jake Freedman right out of her head.

Stay strong...

Oh, yes, she would. She had to. Nobody was going to wreck her life; not her father, not Jake, not any man. This steadfast determination carried her through dinner, sharpening her wits enough to dilute her father's barbs with good-humoured replies. It also formed her resolution when she returned to her bedroom and was faced with the photographs again.

She scooped them up and shoved them straight back into the envelope her father had left with them. It was a blank envelope and she wrote Jake's address on it, grimly pleased that the search for his house had not been completely wasted time. She wanted him to know that she knew about his other woman and he would not be sucking up any more of her time.

To underline that fact, she wrote an accompanying note—

As for any future meeting between us, you can whistle for me, Jake. I'm moving on. Laura.

No angst in those words. She liked the *whistle* bit. It carried a flippant tone, as well as implying he was just another jerk to be ignored.

Having slipped the note into the envelope, she sealed it and put it in her briefcase to be posted tomorrow. Over and done with. Her life was her own again.

Jake sorted his mail, frowning over the business-size envelope with the handwritten address. It wasn't standard practice to hand-write anything that wasn't personal these days. Curious about its content, he slit it open and drew out the photographs and the damning little note from Laura.

A lead weight settled on his heart.

He'd been sucked in by the dancer at the gym. She'd been Costarella's tool. That was bleeding obvious now. He hadn't suspected a set-up when she'd grabbed at him as he was leaving the gym, expressing what seemed like genuine fear of being stalked and pleading with him to walk her home—just a few blocks to where she knew she'd be safe. It wasn't much to ask, wasn't much to do—a random act of kindness that was coming back to spike him with a vengeance.

Then the embrace of gushing gratitude a week later, an over-the-top carry-on that he'd backed away from, not wanting it, not liking it, certainly not encouraging any further involvement with the woman. But that didn't show in the photograph. It didn't serve Costarella's purpose to give Laura shots of his reaction.

He carried the mail into his house, despondently dumping it on the kitchen bench on his way to the small backyard, which provided a sunny haven from the rest of the world. He slumped into one of the deck chairs he'd set out there, still holding Laura's note that brought their journey to a dead end.

He stared at the words—*I'm moving on.*

It was what he had meant her to do, advised her to do, and most probably it was the best course to chop him completely out of her life. Costarella was not about to tolerate any future connection between them. Even if he explained this photographic set-up to Laura and she believed him, Costarella would look for other ways and means to drive wedges into their relationship. It gave him a focus for getting back at Jake for bringing him down and he'd relish that malicious power.

Definitely best that what he'd had with Laura ended here and now.

No future.

He folded the note and tucked it into his shirt pocket.

He'd known all along that this was how it would have to be, but it was still damned difficult to accept. Achieving what he'd set out to do to Alex Costarella felt strangely empty. Like his life after his mother and stepfather had died. But he'd picked himself up then and moved forward. He could do it again.

There should have been warmth in the sunshine.

He couldn't feel it.

The emptiness inside him was very cold.

CHAPTER THIRTEEN

FOR the rest of the year Laura applied herself so thoroughly to her uni course, she not only attained her degree, but also graduated with honours in every subject. This gave her an extra edge over other students entering the workforce for the first time. She was snapped up by a firm of architects, wanting a landscape specialist to enhance their designs. It was a wonderful buoyant feeling to know all her hard work had paid off and she was actually going to begin her chosen career.

The phone call notifying her of her successful interview came in the first week of December and her new employers wanted her in their office the following Monday. After revelling in the news for a few moments, she rushed out to the back garden to tell her mother, who was trailing after Nick Jeffries as he checked the sprinkler system.

'Mum! I got it! The job I interviewed for!' she called out, causing both of them to turn and give her their attention. She grinned exultantly at them as she added, 'And they want me to start next week!'

Her mother's face lit with pleasure. 'That's fantastic, Laura!'

'Fantastic!' Nick repeated, grinning delight at her. 'Congratulations!'

'And before Christmas, too,' her mother said with an air of relief, turning her face up to Nick's and touching his arm in an oddly familiar manner. 'Can we do it?'

He nodded. 'The sooner, the better.'

'Do what?' Laura asked, bemused by what seemed like an intimate flow of understanding between them.

Nick tucked her mother's arm around his and

they faced Laura together as he told her their news. 'Your mother is leaving your father and moving in with me. We've just been waiting for you to have some freedom of choice, Laura, and now you're set.'

She was totally thunderstruck. Her mother and Nick? She had never imagined, never suspected there was anything beyond a casual affection between them, born out of sharing the pleasure of a lovely garden. She knew Nick was a widower, had been for years, but he'd always been very respectful to her mother, caring about what she wanted but never taking liberties that might not be welcome. When had their relationship moved to a different level?

'I can see you're shocked,' her mother said on a deflated sigh.

Her air of disappointment jolted Laura into a quick protest. 'No! No! Just surprised! And pleased,' she quickly added, beaming a smile at both of them.

'It's not good for Alicia here,' Nick said, appealing for her understanding.

That was the understatement of the year!

'I'm sure Mum will be a lot happier with you than with Dad,' Laura said with feeling. 'Both Eddie and I have always liked you, Nick. And appreciated how much you've lightened Mum's life. I think it's brilliant that you're stepping in and taking her away, but I've got to warn you, Dad's bound to be horribly mean about it. He's not a good loser.'

Which was another huge understatement.

Nick patted her mother's hand reassuringly. 'Alicia doesn't need to take anything from him. I can provide for her.'

'There's very little I want to take from this life, Laura. Nick can fit it into his van,' her mother said, looking brighter now that her decision had been so readily accepted by her daughter. 'But you'll have to move on the same day. Either come with us or go to Eddie's until you can afford a place of your own. I can't leave you here, not with your father finding out I've walked out on him.'

'No, that would not be a good scene,' Laura heartily agreed.

The biggest understatement of all!

'I'll go to Eddie's, let you two start your lives together on your own,' she decided. 'It won't be for long. As soon as I get my first pay cheque, I'll look around for an apartment close to my work.'

'We must tell Eddie now,' her mother said anxiously, looking to Nick for his support again.

'Yes, he has to be brought into the plan,' Nick agreed.

'No problem. I'll call him, let him know,' Laura suggested. 'And don't worry, Mum. Eddie will be all for it.'

She shook her head. 'I must tell him, dear. It's only right.'

'Okay. Just trying to save you trouble, Mum.'

'I know. It's what you've been doing for years,' she said sadly. 'But no more, Laura.'

'That's my job from now on,' Nick said with a cheerful grin. 'All you have to do, Laura, is choose what you want to take with you, pack it up and be ready when Alicia nominates the day.'

'A day when I'm sure your father will be out. I'm not going to face him with this. I'll leave him a letter. Let him rage to an empty house.'

'Best course,' Nick said decisively. 'I wouldn't put it past him to stoop to physical violence and I won't have Alicia subjected to any risk of that.'

'Definitely the best course,' Laura agreed. 'What about Friday, Mum? I'm sure Dad said that was when he was meeting with his barrister to plan the counter-attack to the accusations against him.'

Give him some dirt on your lover-boy, Laura,

he'd jeered. *Jake Freedman won't come out of this clean, I can promise you that.*

None of my business, Laura had firmly recited to herself, determined not to encourage her father into elaborating on *the dirt,* refusing to go anywhere that involved Jake. Despite all the intervening months, she hadn't been able to bury the hurt of her disillusionment with him and it was quite impossible to become interested in any other man.

'Yes, Friday!' her mother cried excitedly.

The day of freedom.

She turned to the man who had opened another door for her. 'No way will Alex miss that meeting, Nick. As soon as he's left the house I'll call you.'

'And I'll be here,' he assured her.

It was really heart-touching seeing the caring for her mother written on Nick's face, seeing her open trust in him. Laura had to clear a lump in her throat before she could speak.

'Now we've got that settled, I'm off to my room to start selecting what I want to take with me. You two can start planning a happy future together.'

She kissed them both on their cheeks and skipped away feeling even more light-hearted at the prospect of her mother's escape to a new life. No more oppressive abuse, no more fear, no more misery. Nick Jeffries was not an impressively handsome, wealthy man, but the kindness running through his veins was obviously more attractive to her mother than anything else.

And maybe that was what she should look for in a man.

Forget Jake Freedman's strong sex appeal.

Forget everything she had loved about him.

There had been no real kindness in him.

A kind man would never have used her as Jake had.

Next week she would be starting a new phase

of her life, leaving everything and everyone connected to her father behind, and that would surely make forgetting Jake easier. She would be busy working her way into her career, forging a path of her own without having to worry about her mother's well-being, and looking forward to a really happy, tension-free Christmas for once!

Joy to the world!

Smiling over the words that had sung through her mind, Laura raced upstairs to her room to start organising the big move. Having perused the contents of her wardrobe, she decided large plastic garbage bags were needed for easy transportation. A lot of old stuff need not be taken. She stared down at the turquoise shoes Jake had called erotic on her first date with him at Neil Perry's Spice Temple. Gorgeous shoes. A gift from her mother. But could she ever wear them again without remembering him, remembering how it had been in the hotel after he'd taken them off?

A knock on her door interrupted the miserable train of thought.

'It's just me,' her mother called.

'Come in,' Laura quickly invited, wanting some private time with her mother, mostly to feel totally assured that going with Nick Jeffries was the right move for her, not an act of desperation or some kind of sacrifice to her children's peace of mind.

'Nick has stacked some boxes in the laundry for us to use,' she said, her blue eyes sparkling with happy anticipation.

'Mum, you are sure about this?' Laura asked earnestly. 'You're not just taking some…some easy way out?'

'No, dear. I'm very sure.' She walked over to the bed and sat on the end of it, looking at Laura with a soft, dreamy expression on her face. 'I lost myself with your father. I want to find the person I could have been and Nick will let me do that. I know I'm different with him and I like the difference. He touches my heart and makes me feel good, Laura, good in a way I've never felt before.'

She'd felt good with Jake until… But this wasn't the time to be thinking of him. She had to *stop* thinking of him. 'That's great, Mum,' she said warmly, giving her an ironic smile. 'I guess I'm still a bit surprised. When did you two open up to each other?'

'It was just after my birthday…'

Tenth of October

'Your father had been particularly nasty to me and I was sitting out on the garden bench near the pool, weeping over my miserable existence, wishing I were dead. Nick had come to work and he found me there. There was no hiding my wretched state and he was so kind, so comforting. We talked and talked.…'

She sighed, shook her head as though it

was too difficult—or too private—to explain, but the reminiscent smile on her face spoke of unexpected pleasure found and treasured. 'Anyhow, the more we talked, the more I realised *I* wanted to be with him, and *he* wanted me to be with him, too. We both believe we can make a beautiful little world together. You can't imagine, Laura. Everything feels so different with Nick. So very different…'

Yes, she could imagine. No problem at all in imagining how it was or how it could be. She pulled her mother up from the bed for a hug. 'I'm so glad for you, Mum. Make sure you tell Eddie all that so he won't worry about you.'

'I will, dear. And you must both come to Nick's house for Christmas. We'll have a lovely celebration of it this year.'

'Mmmh…' Laura grinned. 'We'll be able to have fun together.'

'Yes, fun!' Her mother seized the concept

with delight and sailed out of the room, no doubt eager to share it with Nick.

Over the next few days Laura and her mother secretly packed what they wanted to take, storing the boxes in Laura's room, where her father never ventured. Eddie was cock-a-hoop about the plan and in total agreement that it be carried out without their father's knowledge, not risking any explosive confrontation.

Friday morning came. Alex Costarella duly left for his meeting. Nick arrived in his van within minutes of the all-clear call. He and Laura packed the boxes and bags into it while her mother removed her personal papers— birth and marriage certificates from her father's safe—and made a last-minute check that nothing important had been missed.

There were absolutely no regrets on driving away from the Mosman mansion. It was like having a huge weight lifted off their hearts. The sense of freedom was so heady they couldn't help laughing at everything said between them. Laura called Eddie on her mobile phone to inform him of their successful escape and he was out on the street waiting for them when they arrived at his apartment block.

They all moved her belongings into his second bedroom and once that task was complete, she and Eddie accompanied their mother and Nick back to the van to say goodbye and wish them well. Oddly enough her mother looked strained as she nervously fingered a large envelope she'd left on the passenger seat, finally thrusting it at Laura.

'I don't know if it's right or wrong to give you this,' she said anxiously. 'It was in your father's safe and I looked into it while I was searching for my papers. It holds more photos of Jake Freedman—ones he didn't show you, Laura. I think he lied about those he did. Lied to drive a wedge between you and Jake, wanting to hurt. He always wanted to hurt when he didn't get his own way. Maybe seeing these will lessen the hurt a bit. I hope so, dear.'

It felt like a knife was twisting in her heart as she took the envelope, but she managed a smile, quickly saying, 'Don't worry, Mum. What's done is done and it's all in the past anyway. Go with Nick now. Be happy.'

They drove off and she stood so long staring blankly after the van, Eddie picked up the vibes of her distress and hugged her shoulders. 'It might be in the past but it's not done with, is it, Laura?' he said sympathetically. 'I know you haven't got over the guy. So let's go inside and look at what Dad's Machiavellian streak came up with to destroy what you had together.'

They were before-and-after photographs— before and after the damning shots that had driven her to reject any future with the man she had loved. Jake hadn't followed the pretty blonde into the house. She'd gone inside alone. Even the shots of them walking down the street together had no hint of any intimacy between them—just a man accompanying a woman.

As for the kiss at the gym, it was clear that the woman had thrown herself at Jake. There were snaps of his face showing surprise, annoyance, impatience, rejection, none of which had been visible in the photo her father had shown her.

'It was a set-up,' Eddie muttered, tapping a clear shot of the blonde. 'I've seen this woman around the traps. She's a fairly high-class working girl. This would have been an easy gig for her and no doubt Dad paid her well for it.'

A set-up…and she'd fallen for it; hook, line and sinker.

'I didn't give Jake a chance to explain,' she said miserably. 'I posted him the incriminating photos with a message that wrote him out of my life.'

'Don't fret it, Laura. I'm sure Jake was smart enough to realise Dad wasn't going to tolerate

a connection between the two of you. He probably thought he was saving you grief by letting
it go.'

Yes, he would think that. But he wouldn't
contact her when the business with her father
was all over. Not now.

'I didn't believe in him enough. I didn't *stay
strong*,' she cried, gutted by her failure of faith
in his caring for her.

Eddie frowned. 'You think there was genuine
feeling for you on his side?'

'Yes! It was just the situation making everything too hard. He promised me we'd meet
again but I've messed it up, Eddie, taking Dad's
word instead of his. I've completely messed it
up!'

'Not necessarily. You must have his home address if you posted the photos to him,' he said
thoughtfully. 'You're free of Dad now, Laura,
and so is Mum. Why not pay Jake a visit, find

out where you stand with him? Better to know than not know.'

'Yes!' She jumped up from her seat at Eddie's table where they had laid out the photographs, gripped by a determination to set everything right, if she could. 'I'll go. It's a chance to nothing, isn't it?'

He nodded. 'If you have to go there, go there.'

She did.

A wild hope zinged through her heart every step of the way, right until the front door of Jake's house was opened and she was faced with a young woman holding a baby on her hip.

'Hello. Are you one of our new neighbours?' the woman asked with bright-eyed interest.

'No, I...I was looking for Jake Freedman,' Laura blurted out.

'Oh, I'm sorry. He's gone, I'm afraid, and I don't have a forwarding address. We bought the house from him two months ago and moved in last week. I have no idea where you can find him.'

'It's okay. Thank you. Have a nice life here.'

A nice life in the house Jake had worked on and sold…and he had now moved on.

And Laura had no idea where to, either.

But it wasn't the absolute end, she told herself on the long trudge back to Paddington. The case against her father was set down to be heard in March next year—three more months away. Jake was the prime witness against him. He had to attend the court hearing, give evidence—fulfil the mission that had driven them apart.

A court of law was a public place.

She could go there.

She would go there.

luck at even catching a glimpse of him, she entered the inquiry room, settling on one of the back seats, sure that she would see him here sometime today.

Her father was seated beside his barrister. He saw her, giving her a bulletlike stare before turning away. She didn't care what he thought of her presence. Only what Jake thought mattered.

The hearing started. Jake had not entered the room. Laura set aside her frustration and listened to the accusations her father had to answer. This was what Jake had been secretly working on—more important to him than their relationship.

Sixteen companies were named—JQE amongst them. Struggling companies that could have been saved by arranging bridging loans but which her father had chosen to bury, gouging millions out of selling off their assets

CHAPTER FOURTEEN

LAURA dressed carefully for the first day of the hearing, choosing to wear the professional black suit she donned for business meetings. She wanted Jake to see her as a fully adult woman, established in her career and capable of standing on her own. However, the suit was figure-hugging, accentuating her feminine curves, and she left her hair loose, wanting him to see her as sexy, too, reminding him of the pleasures they had shared.

She had all week to make contact with him, having arranged for the time off work, but her heart was set on sooner rather than later. Arriving early at the court house, she tensely searched the waiting rooms and corridors, hoping to cross paths with Jake. Having no by charging outrageous fees for his services as liquidator.

The judge described it as 'Churning and burning.'

The day dragged on with no sight of Jake, not in the morning session, not in the lunch-break, not in the afternoon session.

Her father was the only witness called. He admitted to earning between four and six million dollars a year from failing companies but belligerently insisted it was by carrying out due process and he was innocent of any wrongdoing. His air of contempt for the court did not endear him to the judge. Laura hated listening to him. She kept darting glances around the room, hoping to see Jake, willing him to appear.

Why wasn't he here?

Surely this was the culmination of his mission for justice.

Shouldn't he be listening to what her father said so he could rebut it?

Jake was sitting in the consultation room, waiting for the prosecuting barrister to report on the afternoon session, feeling buoyantly confident that Alex Costarella would finally be nailed for the fraudulent bastard he was. The glass panels of the door gave him a view of the area directly outside the enquiry room. A rush of people into it signalled that the session was over.

Jake recognised the reporters who had tried to interview him. The case was drawing quite a bit of interest from the business sector of the media. Which was good. Too much skulduggery was hidden from the public. The more people were aware of what went on, the more they could guard against it, or at least question what was happening.

Laura!

Jake bolted to his feet, shocked at seeing her amongst the departing spectators, his mind instantly torn by uncertainty over what she was doing here and the wild urge to stride out and sweep her into a fiercely possessive embrace. It had been so long—almost a year—but just the sight of her had his body buzzing with the need to have her again.

She looked stunning, the black suit barely confining her voluptuous curves, her glorious hair bouncing around her shoulders. His fingers itched to rake through its silky mass. His groin was tingling hotly from a swift rush of blood. He'd never wanted a woman so much. If he reached out to her now, would she happily respond, or…?

More likely she would spurn him, he realised, the surge of excitement draining slowly away. Given that she had believed whatever story her father had spun around the photographs she'd sent him, no doubt believing she'd been used as a malicious thrill on the side, as well, the probability was she was here to support her father against him.

Love…hate—they could colour anyone's judgement.

He watched her join the group of people waiting for the elevator, watched her until steel doors closed behind her, and ached inside for what had been lost. He'd let the past rule his decisions, the long-burning need for justice. It was a crusade for good over evil, yet he knew he would feel no joy in the victory. Satisfaction, perhaps, but no joy.

He had to take the witness stand tomorrow. If Laura attended the hearing again… A violent determination rampaged through him. He would make her believe every word he said, every revelation of the kind of man her father was. It might not win him anything from her on a personal level, but at least she wouldn't be able to sustain any support for her rotten father, who had ruined any chance they might have had for a future together.

The second day...

Laura had no sooner settled on a back-row seat in the inquiry room than her father was on his feet, pushing back the chair he had occupied at his barrister's table so violently it tumbled over. He ignored it, glaring furiously at her as he strode down the aisle, obviously intent on confrontation.

She sat tight, steeling herself to ride out his wrath. Since she and her mother had left the Mosman mansion before Christmas, none of the family had had any personal contact with him. No doubt he contemptuously considered them rats that had deserted the sinking ship, but he had no power over them anymore. He couldn't actually *do* anything to her, not here in public, but if looks could kill, she'd certainly be dead.

'What the hell are you doing here?' he demanded, the thunderous tone of voice promising punishment for her sins against him.

'Listening,' she answered curtly, refusing to be cowed.

Burning hatred in his eyes. 'Are you on with Jake Freedman again?'

'No.'

His lips curled in a sneer. 'Chasing after him.'

She met his vicious mockery with absolute self-determination. 'You lied to me about him, Dad. I've come to hear the truth.'

'Truth!' he scoffed. 'You benefited from his stepfather's fall. That's the truth. And Freedman isn't about to forget it, not when he's been brooding over it for years.'

The judge's entrance demanded her father's return to his barrister's side. Laura was shaken by the encounter. She'd been all keyed up, hoping that a meeting with Jake might lead to a resumption of their relationship. Fixated on the photographs, she hadn't given any thought to other factors. When all was said and done, she was still her father's daughter, and Jake may well have killed any feeling he'd had for her and moved on, especially after she'd used false evidence to blow him away.

A chance to nothing, she'd said to Eddie, and the truth was she was probably fooling herself about having any chance at all. She sat in a slump of silent despair, not hearing anything until Jake's name was called.

Tension instantly stiffened her spine and pressed her legs tightly together. Her eyes automatically drank in everything about him as he entered the room and was led to the witness box. He wore a sober grey suit and the air of a man all primed to carry out deadly business. James Bond—sleek, sophisticated, sexy, making her heart kick at how handsome he was, making her stomach flutter at how devastating this day could be to her. Even the sound of his voice as he was sworn in evoked memories of intimate moments, making her ache for more.

He shot his gaze around the room before sitting down. For one electric moment it stopped on her. There was no smile, not the slightest change of expression on his face at seeing her. She didn't smile at him, either. The feelings inside her were too intense. She fiercely willed him to know she was here for him. The moment passed all too quickly, his gaze flicking to the prosecuting barrister as he settled on his chair.

He didn't look at her again.

Not once.

Laura listened to his testimony, hearing a biting edge in every word. It became perfectly clear that her father's intent as a liquidator was exploitation, without any regard to the interests of any company or its creditors. Billable hours extended to clerical staff, even to the tea and coffee lady—each at three hundred dollars an hour. At one meeting with creditors, the coffee served to them came to eighty dollars a cup.

'Nice cup,' the judge remarked acidly.

'Not exactly sweet when the creditors never get their entitlements,' Jake said just as acidly.

The flow of evidence went on and on, backed up by facts and figures that could not be denied. They painted a picture of shocking corruption. Laura felt ashamed of her connection to the man who hadn't cared how many people he hurt in amassing more and more money for himself. She'd known he had a cruel nature. She hadn't known his contempt for others extended so far.

It was sickening.

She understood now how much this mission had meant to Jake, especially given what had happened with his parents. Apart from the personal element, it was right to take her father down, saving others from suffering similar situations. He was doing good, more good than she had ever done in her life, showing up the faults of a system that was a feeding ground for liquidators without any conscience.

It took a big person to stand up and blow the whistle on it, regardless of any cost to himself. She admired Jake's drive to get it done. But her father was right about one thing. She was his daughter and her life had been cushioned in the luxury of his greedy profiteering. It wasn't her fault but she was definitely tainted by it in Jake's mind.

I don't want to want you.

And there was no sign of him wanting her now. He wouldn't even look at her, though she had been willing him to all day. He probably hated the sight of her—a memory of weakness on his part, not to be revisited.

Stay strong.

His whole demeanour, his voice, his laying out of undeniable facts, had been relentlessly strong today. He was not going to reconnect with her. Laura slipped out of the inquiry room as soon as the afternoon session ended, carrying the misery of lost hope with her. There was no point in coming back tomorrow. Jake had obviously shut the door on her and she must now do it on him.

She forced her legs to walk straight to the elevator, forced her finger to jab the *down* button. Other people clustered around her, waiting for the elevator to arrive. Minutes crawled by. There was a buzz of voices commenting on the hearing. Laura heard her father called *one hell of a shark*. No sympathy for him. Nor should there be.

Her own heart suddenly rebelled against leaving Jake believing that she had been here to support her father. The elevator doors opened. The surge forward carried her into the compartment but she wriggled out again, telling herself there was one last stand she had to make—a matter of self-respect if nothing else.

Jake emerged from the inquiry room with his barrister, the two men conferring with each other as they walked out. Laura didn't care if she would be interrupting something important. What she had to say would only take a couple of moments and it was important to her. Her hands clenched in determination. Her chin instinctively lifted. Every nerve in her body was wire-tight as she closed the short distance between them.

As though sensing her approach, Jake's head jerked towards her. His gaze locked on hers, hard and uninviting, twin dark bolts boring into her head. The barrister murmured something to him. Jake's hand sliced a sharp dismissive gesture, his attention not wavering from Laura. She stopped a metre short of him, close enough to be heard, her mind totally focussed on delivering a few last words.

'I found out that my father lied about the photographs. I'm sorry that I let him influence my belief in you, Jake. I wish you well.'

That was it.

She turned and walked back to the elevator where another group of people had gathered, waiting for its return. She could go now, having righted the wrong she had done Jake. And she did wish him well. He was a good man.

She didn't hate him!

The steel guard Jake had put around his feelings for Laura Costarella cracked wide open at this stunning realisation. He was in instant tumult over her apology, wanting to know more, but she had already turned away and was heading for the elevator, not waiting for any response from him. What did that mean? She didn't want one? Didn't expect one?

How long had she known about her father's lie? If it was before this hearing, she wouldn't have attended it to support him. Was it simply curiosity that had drawn her here, a need to know everything that had limited their relationship and made it so impossible to sustain? But surely she wouldn't have bothered unless... she still had feelings for him.

I wish you well....

It was a goodbye line.

He didn't want it to be. He wanted...

The elevator doors opened. Laura was following the group of people into it. She was going and everything within him violently rebelled against letting her go.

Without any conscious thought at all he lifted two fingers to his lips and whistled the most piercing whistle he'd ever produced in his life.

CHAPTER FIFTEEN

THE whistle startled everyone who heard it. Conversations were momentarily cut off. Feet stopped moving. Heads turned. Laura's heart felt as though it had been kicked. Her mind instantly recalled the kiss-off line she'd written to Jake.

As for any future meeting between us, you can whistle for me.

Had he done it?

Please…let it be him wanting a meeting with her.

A meeting with a future in mind.

The other people resumed their movement into the elevator. Laura didn't. She had to turn around, had to see. If it was Jake who had whistled, he'd be looking at her, perhaps holding out a hand in an appeal for her to stay where she was, wait a minute.

A chance to nothing, she told herself, her heart hammering as she acted on her need to know, throwing a quick glance over her shoulder. Jake had left his barrister's side and was striding towards her, determined purpose burning in the eyes that locked onto hers, holding her still until he could reach her.

The elevator doors closed. Laura was the only person left behind. But Jake was coming to her. They hadn't talked to each other for almost a year. She had no idea what was on his mind, yet the leap of hope in hers was so strong, it was impossible to put a guard of caution around it. He could probably see it in her eyes, the wanting, the needing. Pride couldn't hide it. She had none where he was concerned.

He stopped about a metre away from her, tension emanating from him, making her nerves even tighter.

'It's been a long time,' he said.

'Yes,' she agreed, the word coming out huskily. Her throat was choked up with a mountain of tumultuous emotions.

'There's a good coffee shop on the corner of the next block. Can I buy you a cappuccino?'

She swallowed hard to get rid of the lump. He was offering time together, wanting time together. A meeting. 'I'd like that very much,' she answered, her voice still furred with feelings that were totally uncontrollable.

'Good!' he said and stepped around her to press the elevator button, summoning it to this floor again.

Third time lucky, Laura thought giddily.

Jake flashed her a smile. 'I wish you well, too, Laura. I always have.'

She nodded, yearning for far more than well-wishing from him.

'Are you still living with your father?' he asked.

'No. I have a full-time job now. Landscape designer for a firm of architects. I can afford my own apartment.'

'What about your mother?'

'She moved out the same time I did. She's okay. Much happier.'

'Sharing your apartment?'

'No. Nick Jeffries, our former handyman/ gardener, carried her off to his home. He's a widower and they're very much in love.'

'Wow!' Jake grinned, surprised and seemingly delighted by this turn of events. 'I guess you don't have to worry about her anymore.'

'No, I don't. Having nothing to fear from Nick, she's already blooming into a far more positive person.'

'That's good. Great!'

He really did look pleased—pleased because he didn't want anyone to be her father's victim, or pleased because she was completely free and clear of any continuing connection with her father? Was he checking to see if he could reasonably resume a relationship with her with no negative fallout from it? Did he want to? She was still her father's daughter. Nothing could change that.

The elevator arrived and Jake waved an invitation to precede him into it. They were the only people occupying the small compartment on this ride. Jake stood silently beside her on the way down. Laura was too conscious of his close presence to think of anything to say. She had been intensely intimate with this man and the memories of it were flooding through her mind—the passionate kisses, the exquisite sensitivity of his touch. She had to press her thighs tightly together to contain the hot, searing need to have him again.

As they walked out to the street she was fiercely wishing he would take hold of her hand but he didn't attempt even that simple physical link with her. The evening rush hour hadn't quite started. The sidewalk wasn't crowded. There was no reason for Jake to take her arm to keep them together and he didn't. They reached the coffee shop without touching at all and Jake led her to a booth, waiting for her to slide in on one bench seat before seating himself across the table from her.

'Like old times,' she remarked, managing an ironic smile to cover the sick feeling that this might be the last time she shared a table with Jake.

He returned the smile. 'A lot of water has passed under the bridge since then. Are you happy with the career you've chosen?'

She nodded. 'It's very challenging but I'm loving it. What about you, Jake? Have you moved on to renovating another house?'

'Yes. I sold the last one.'

'I know.'

He looked quizzically at her and she flushed, realising she had given away the fact that she

had tried to visit him. Too late to take back those revealing words. She heaved a sigh to relieve the tightness in her chest and plunged into telling the truth. What point was there in holding back?

'On the day we left Mosman—it was just before last Christmas—Mum found a bunch of other photographs of you in Dad's safe. They made me realise he'd set you up, then spun a false story to make me believe…' She hesitated, inwardly recoiling from repeating the horribly demeaning picture her father had drawn.

'That I was a liar and a cheat,' Jake finished for her with a wry grimace. 'I didn't blame you for believing him, Laura. It was my fault. I should never have touched you. It put you in a rotten position when I made my move against him.'

His use of the past tense hurt. If he regretted their relationship, what hope was there for a future one? But she was halfway through her explanation and she wanted to finish it.

'Anyhow, it made me feel really bad about how I'd completely written you off, so I went to your house at Woollahra, wanting to apologise, except you were gone and other people had moved in. I had no means of contact with you unless I came to the hearing, and I'm glad I did. Listening to everything being laid out made me understand why you had to take my father down. You were right to do it. And I do wish you well, Jake.'

There!

Definitely water under the bridge now!

And she'd managed it with reasonable dignity.

A waiter arrived to take their order and Jake asked for two cappuccinos, quickly inquiring if she wanted something to eat as well—a toasted sandwich? Laura shook her head. Her stomach was in knots. After the waiter had left them, Jake regarded her seriously for several moments, making the knots even tighter.

'It's not over, Laura,' he said quietly. 'There will be ugly things said about me in the days to come.'

The dirt her father had up his sleeve.

'Will they be true?' she asked.

'Not on any professional level. He can't deny the evidence against him. It's too iron-tight. So I'm confident that nothing will change the eventual outcome. He's gone from the industry, regardless of what he uses in an attempt to discredit me.'

'Do you know what he'll try to use?'

He made a wry grimace. 'You were my only weakness, Laura. I'm anticipating an attack on my character revolving around my involvement with you.'

She frowned. 'But that had nothing to do with how he ran his business.'

'I think he'll try to link it up.'

A fierce rebellion swept through Laura. Her father had been too successful in hurting others, deliberately doing it and taking malicious pleasure in it. She wanted him to fail for once, and be shown up as the liar he was—some justice for the months of misery he'd given her.

She leaned forward, earnestly pressing for Jake to agree with her. 'I've taken this week off work. I could testify on your behalf. I know you didn't do me any wrong, Jake.'

His face tightened in instant rejection. 'This isn't your war, Laura. It was wrong of me to put you in the line of fire and I won't do it again. I'll ride it through.'

'It *is* my war,' she cried vehemently. 'I've taken the bullets and I want to return them. I'm not ashamed of my involvement with you. It makes a much stronger stand if we ride this through together. Publicly together. Surely you can see that any capital my father might think he could make out of our connection becomes utter nonsense if we're still connected.'

He didn't offer any quick rebuttal this time. The riveting dark eyes scoured hers with blazing intensity. Laura had the sinking feeling he was unsure of her staying power. She hadn't remained strong against her father's manipulation in the past.

'There's no other man in your life, Laura?' he asked quietly.

The question startled her—not what she had been expecting. It offered hope that Jake was considering her suggestion. 'No. I'm free and clear,' she stated firmly.

It suddenly occurred to her that he might not be. He hadn't touched her. Just because the memory of him had made her disinterested in other men didn't mean he'd felt a similar detachment. She'd certainly opened the door for him to move on when she'd shut it on her life.

'I'm sorry. I didn't think,' she blurted out,

flushing self-consciously over her single-mindedness, her hands fluttering an apologetic dismissal of her impulsive ideas. 'If you're in another relationship, of course this won't work.'

'I'm not,' he said swiftly, reaching across the table to take one of her hands in his, long strong fingers stroking, soothing her agitation. 'There's nothing I'd like more than to be connected to you again, Laura. I just want to be sure it's right for you.'

A wild joy burst through her heart. She stared at him, scarcely able to believe she did have another chance with him. Warmth from his touch ran up her arm and spread through her entire body, a blissful warmth, promising her the loving she craved. She wanted this man so much, yet it hadn't really been right for her before, not with him limiting their relationship to great dinners and great sex. The temptation to take whatever she could of him played through her mind, but she knew that would never be enough.

'Will you show me the house you're now working on?'

It was a critical question, challenging how much he wanted to be connected to her.

His face relaxed into a smile, his eyes twinkling sexy delight. 'Would after we drink our coffee be too soon?'

She laughed in sheer ecstatic relief. 'No, not too soon. Where is it?'

'Petersham. It's about ten minutes in the train from Town Hall, then a short walk from the station. An easy commute to the city centre.'

'Is it another terrace house?'

'No. A two-bedroom cottage with a yard, both of which have been neglected for years.' He grinned. 'Maybe you can give me some ideas on what to do with the yard.'

It was so wonderful that he was willing to share this project with her, she grinned straight back. 'I'd love to design a cottage garden. Something delightfully old-fashioned. All I've done so far at work is very modern landscape.'

'Then you'll have to go shopping for plants with me,' he said decisively. 'Guide me into buying the best.'

More sharing. Laura's cup of happiness was suddenly bubbling to the brim. 'No problem,' she assured him, revelling in allowing herself to love this man all over again.

The waiter returned with their cappuccinos. Jake released her hand and they sat apart again, but another journey had begun—one that shimmered with the promise of far more than the first they'd taken together. Laura couldn't remember a coffee ever tasting so good.

Jake could scarcely believe this incredibly fortunate turn of events. Laura hadn't moved on. Not from him. And the time apart had not been wasted. She had achieved complete independence from her father and quite clearly would never allow herself to be subjected to his influence again. It was now totally irrelevant that she was Alex Costarella's daughter. She was simply herself—the beautiful, strong, giving woman he had come to love. And since her mother no longer needed her in any protective sense, the way ahead for them was free of any insurmountable complications.

He could throw caution to the winds, share whatever he wanted with Laura without any sense of guilt over how hurt she might be from associating with him. The whole truth was out in the open now. There was no reason to hold back on anything. Where the future might take them as a couple was entirely in their own hands. The most important thing was he could have her again. Nothing else really mattered.

Froth from the cappuccino coated her upper lip. He wanted to lick it off. Her tongue slid out and swept it away. Her beautiful blue eyes twinkled at him teasingly as though she knew what he'd been thinking.

'I haven't wanted any woman since you, Laura,' he said softly. That was the truth, too, and he needed her to know it. The damning photographs could have left doubts in her mind about how deeply he'd felt connected to her. This was a new start and he couldn't bear anything marring it.

She smiled, happiness lighting up her lovely face. 'It's been the same for me, too, Jake, though I did have a lot of bad thoughts about you.'

'The woman in the photographs…she said she was being stalked and pleaded with me to walk her home from the gym. It was an act of kindness, Laura, nothing more.'

The smile broadened. 'I like kindness in a man. Nick is very kind to Mum. She never had that from Dad.'

Neither did you. Only demands and abuse if they weren't met.

Jake understood where Laura was coming from, why marriage was not an attractive proposition to her, but maybe he could change her view of it, given enough time together. She was certainly seeing the difference for her mother.

He wanted a family in his future. The loss of it had driven him all these years and now that the goal he had set himself had been reached, he could plan a different scenario for his life, hopefully with Laura. It was like a miracle that it was possible at all.

She put down her cup and gave him a look of eager anticipation. 'Are we done here? Ready to go?'

Desire roared through him like an express train. He couldn't get her out of the coffee shop fast enough. They started the walk towards Town Hall hand in hand, a joyous bounce in their step. It was rush hour, people crowding past them either way. They came to a building with a recessed entrance and Jake instantly pulled Laura out of the mêlée on the sidewalk and into his embrace against a sheltered side wall.

'I've been wanting to do this ever since I saw you yesterday,' he murmured, his eyes blazing with naked need.

'Yesterday?' she echoed quizzically.

'I thought you'd come for your father. If I'd known you'd come for me…'

He couldn't wait. Like in the garden the first day they'd met, like on their first date on the way to the hotel…he had to kiss her and she wrapped her arms around his neck and kissed him right back, their passion for each other as wildly exhilarating as ever, more so with the freedom from all restrictions.

But they couldn't give it full expression in this public place.

They had to move on.
And they did.
Together.

* * * * *

Mills & Boon® Large Print
February 2012

THE MOST COVETED PRIZE
Penny Jordan

THE COSTARELLA CONQUEST
Emma Darcy

THE NIGHT THAT CHANGED EVERYTHING
Anne McAllister

CRAVING THE FORBIDDEN
India Grey

HER ITALIAN SOLDIER
Rebecca Winters

THE LONESOME RANCHER
Patricia Thayer

NIKKI AND THE LONE WOLF
Marion Lennox

MARDIE AND THE CITY SURGEON
Marion Lennox

THE POWER OF VASILII
Penny Jordan

THE REAL RIO D'AQUILA
Sandra Marton

A SHAMEFUL CONSEQUENCE
Carol Marinelli

A DANGEROUS INFATUATION
Chantelle Shaw

HOW A COWBOY STOLE HER HEART
Donna Alward

TALL, DARK, TEXAS RANGER
Patricia Thayer

THE BOY IS BACK IN TOWN
Nina Harrington

JUST AN ORDINARY GIRL?
Jackie Braun

0212 Rom LP